# Reflections on Love

MIGUEL A. SANJOAQUIN

Copyright © 2020 Miguel A. SanJoaquin

All rights reserved.

*December 21, 2010*
*Washington, D.C.*

*Dear Gipani,*
*This letter is a long-announced goodbye.*
*The truth is that I don't know how to let you go… neither you, nor love itself. But what is love? We spend half a lifetime trying to answer this key question of our very existence: What is love?*

*We write songs infused with love, we make verses that bleed with love, we contemplate sunsets invented to make love. We meander uncertainly through life, trusting in the call of love. We dodge storms and flurries, and we do it out of love. We cross deserts devoid of emotion, trusting that at the other end we might find love. We let candles be consumed for love, let the heart beat unrestrained for love, let the soul suffer love. People are born from making love, they live by and for love, and they die when love ends. We feel enlightened by the flame of love, and, sometimes, we are even blinded by an excess of love. We love each other for love, and we even hate each other for love. We enjoy life, we feel, and we suffer because of love. And yet, after recognizing that almost everything is touched by the tentacle of love, that a great part of what happens in life is due to love, in the end, the truth is that we don't have the slightest idea of what love is all about —what to do with it, and even more important, how to keep it alive.*

*When I met you, I thought I had found the answer, learned what love is, or rather, I thought I had found love itself. But today, as I write this farewell letter, when sadly that door is closing to us, I think I understand that love as a tangible concept doesn't exist. It exists perhaps as an ephemeral concept, as a definition of a sensation, always transitory, that keeps transforming. And, for that reason, perhaps we never manage to capture its absolute essence or to understand it. I now think of love as four stages of the soul, like four seasons, with the heart wandering in their wake: falling in love, being in love, loving, and having loved.*

*The first stage —falling in love— is so evanescent and brief that it can't even be categorized as a tangible concept, and therefore it remains transient. It's like an explosive spring, the awakening of the senses, an enchantment, or something similar, in which you live floating on reality. It's something magical, a powerful narcotic that gives you powers that exceed your very limits, making you feel capable of conquering the whole world. It's a feeling that controls you, and that you let yourself be controlled by, because you know that, unfortunately, it will pass, and then you will be left abandoned, lifeless, waiting for the next dose of love to arrive, bringing you back to life. It's a feeling based on irrational parameters, on poorly understood chemicals, where there is no common sense because it is a unique and irreplaceable moment in which being irrational is precisely what is valid (and the opposite, an irrationality). Besides, you will have the rest of your life for using common sense.*

*This is the moment in which you allow yourself to slide through a greased tunnel of love, not knowing if at the end of that tunnel there will be light or not. But who cares!? At the end of the day, the really wonderful part of it is to glide fleetingly, light as a goose feather. It is simply a wonderful state of mind, a Ferris wheel we want to ride again and again. It is an illusory state housed in limbo, during which you wait for reality to dictate whether it is appropriate for this feeling to evolve or die.*

*For us, this moment occurred when you and I met by chance in the middle of the countryside in Oxfordshire, and, instantly, we both wanted to invent an excuse never to separate. This is when we gazed feverishly into each other's eyes as we circled the world while drinking endless pints at the Eagle & Child. This is when I closed my eyes and I continued to see that your silky, jet-black hair matches your eyes: two enormous lagoons of mysterious darkness. This is also when your turquoise nails made me foresee the future, a future we would experience years later while we visited the salty desert of Uyuni, where I would remember with nostalgia the past paradoxes of life.*

*But here —in that first stage— I was happy making you laugh non-stop, because I thought laughter, not words, is the most powerful weapon for conquering the soul. We never paid attention to time because time was ours. We didn't need to play any music in the background because it resonated through our bodies. You never said no to one more glass of wine because we were already drunk with love. This is where I would have stayed a lifetime. But, unfortunately, we couldn't, because in this time-constrained state of mind, when the bell rings, one has to evolve, irreversibly, to the next stage.*

*In this second stage —"being in love," or the summer of love— lovers continue to enjoy the warmth of the moment, although some of those initially rowdy birds start to chirp more quietly. During this phase, happiness spreads throughout the body like an analgesic, and you feel safe from all pain. Roots begin to grow from no one knows where, and no one knows how or why, but, little by little, they reach the other, achieving the perhaps fictitious but wonderful feeling of being a single organism.*

*At this point for us, our walks became eternal, conversations infinite, and desire limitless. For the first time, we spoke of "us" and we fell into a deep silence, followed by your head on my shoulder and the first mention of "what if..." Although a sudden fear made me pause, I finally took the risk and asked, "What if we lived together for the rest of our lives."*

*You looked me in the eye and, with astonishing sincerity, said, "I would."*

*It wasn't your words but their promptness that made me unequivocally know that this was the way it was meant to be, and so it was.*

*This is when we traveled to Africa for the first time, and, again, the fleeting thought of making that a lifelong project—as we eventually did—actually crossed our minds, because our visions never remained mere chimeras. Our mighty love always took care of turning our visions into reality. ("If we believe...," we used to say. Remember?)*

*The third phase comes: loving. This is an autumn, a period of deceleration in all its forms, during which the senses begin to recover from the shocks and agitation of the previous seasons, and when feelings find themselves more anchored to reality, although the passion still exists. Here the sea becomes peaceful and you navigate calmly, without feeling the pressure of breaking the silence with unnecessary words already said or laughs that had already been laughed. Here you allow yourself to look around inside that quiet ocean and think again about your own things, gifting with a gentle smile to that other rower who rows alongside in the same boat and who responds with equal moderation and contentment.*

*The music that plays in the background is no longer a verbena —it is still of celebration, yes— but now that melody is more like a waltz, an elegant waltz where you do not suffer from arrhythmias or spasms like during that, now bygone, first dance. And when the dance is over, you look at the other and say non-sophisticated things like "What a nice evening."*

*During our third phase, concerns of a more practical nature arose, and gradually invaded all, leaving us without much room for conversation about those other less practical things that previously fed our evenings and hand-in-hand walks.*

*But it was fine! It was fine because we still had plenty of pure love accumulated from past seasons to live from (or so we believed).*

*Besides, we were building a life project, and life itself is also full of practical aspects that one must accept: domestic things, finance, mortgages, and other cumbersome numbers. All a piece of shit, yes, but necessary. Never mind, because we still feel love for the other and, with that, you can move any heavy stones —rearrange the furniture as well, which sometimes weighs as much or even more than those very same stones.*

*Finally, the time comes when you love silently: the winter of glowing feelings. Time —in some cases that so-called contract named* marriage— *generates the (false) perception of a sentimental monopoly and exclusivity, where you (again falsely) feel protected and accommodated. Perhaps as a consequence, you make the strategic mistake of thinking certain things are no longer needed, like cosmetic care (as it should be) or asking for things gently (as it should be), where you think that you can simply turn around in bed and fall asleep with total impunity, without giving or longing for that magical goodnight kiss (as it should be). This is the phase during which the timber of that massive wardrobe in which love is stored is stripped of all varnish, until one day you sit in front of it and mutter: "We should have refurbished this furniture ages ago..."*

*But it doesn't matter. It still doesn't matter. Because you're certain of one thing: that you would give up your own life for the other. And that is worth everything! From now on, that becomes the ultimate test for measuring the robustness of love. Those past parameters, such as how many times you made love per week, or how many passionate kisses you gave or received, become an obsolete metric. Now, giving your own life for the other is the irrefutable proof of that recycled love. To give your own life for the other... What a paradox... You feel perfectly capable of such tremendous sacrifice while failing to attend to much easier needs. "You can't have everything," you tell yourself encouragingly. And it's actually true: you can't have the four seasons in one (love is not a pizza).*

*We reached this fourth stage when you and I —already living in Washington D.C.— sat on the sofa at home, you watching your favorite series, me listening to the radio (with my headphones to avoid disturbing you), and we used to say things like, "Do you remember that tomorrow I'm going on a trip for two weeks?" which meant "Let's go to bed and have sex". Here is perhaps where we made the strategic mistake of thinking that everything that had to be conquered had already been conquered. What a fatal mistake in the game of love… It was snowing over us, and, by the time we noticed, we were so snowed under that the cold had spread everywhere, even to our very hearts.*

*But not everything was bad. There was also glory in that winter, of course. We had times of pausing, of looking back, and, contemplating the long trail of battles waged —almost all of them won— we boasted of our heroic achievements. We admired all the castles built and told ourselves, "Look at what we did together."*

*The truth is that that was indeed the case… And if one manages —and this is a conditional if— to come to terms with the fact that those four seasons not only arrive but also pass (irremediably), if one realizes that one can't fight against nature and that the most one can aspire to is to add some sunshine to that cold period, and to plant a few exogenous tulips so that the winter has more color and is less gray, then… who in their right mind should not feel happy to complete those four cycles of love? Who should not feel fortunate to reach the maturity of love? Who!?*

*And yet, there is a factor, an unpredictable and uncontrollable feeling, a human weakness —too human, perhaps— that can put everything at risk: that one day, one random day, one sits under that robust tree of love —bare of any leaves now— and one makes the fatal mistake of confessing to oneself, "I miss the spring."*

*Signed,*
*Me*

# CHAPTER ONE

## DAYS IN OXFORD

It happened during the first trimester —that of Michaelmas— when the leaves turn the color of ripe cherries before falling over the Isis, when students wearing wellies stroll across Port Meadow searching for autumn, when the rowing season begins and the new challenges too. Yes, it was in the trimester of Michaelmas, when the glasses in the Eagle & Child are filled with mulled wine that evaporates, carrying cinnamon with it and intoxicating the soul with a fantastic realism and the heart with real fantasies; when new hands greet old hands and old hands say goodbye to others that have become even older. Yes, it was during Michaelmas that I fell in love with you, and you thought you had fallen in love with me.

We met on a gloomy October afternoon, under a leaden gray sky, the most colorful day of my life. After another false summer in Oxford, the rains had left puddles here and there. Vast islands of grass were growing out of control, and rotten leaves were piling up everywhere, giving Port Meadow a sense of wonderful carelessness. It was one of those days one misjudges as simply another day--just before one's life changes forever. I remember how the training boats were plowing the river like agile dolphins when, suddenly, I saw you for the first time. You ran along the riverside shouting like crazy to the students, "Come on, you bastards!" while ranting whole paragraphs of Winston Churchill's most fervent war-time speeches, which you mixed with other celebrated phrases used by Roman generals to inspire their troops in the Germanic campaigns. And the worst part is that you did it in a terrible, put-on British accent, which I later discovered you were convinced was perfect, even though it was beautifully contaminated by your incorrigible Spanish accent.

Judging by your speech and pronunciation, I presumed that you would be new at Uni, the beneficiary of a scholarship for foreigners that I assumed you had won by pure chance. I don't know why, but for some strange reason I anticipated that you would be one of those Spanish guys who unload their full arsenal of sweet words and lingering glances on a person, leaving you doubting whether any truth hid behind all that talk. I was also convinced you would have spent the whole summer tumbling from pub to pub, drinking lager until dawn, and spending your entire stipend in the company of friends of dubious reputation. My hunches were right, except one: you preferred to drink bitter.

You looked like a runaway colt those boats: alienated, muddied, like a beast cantering across the meadow, chasing your own invisible goal, which is actually what always made you so special. When you tripped over me, or rather, when you bulldozed into me in the middle of your delirium, you looked me in the eye (as if inspecting me), and after observing my second-hand Raleigh brand bicycle, you uttered your first sentence. "Wolfson versus Wolfson: Wolfson always wins."

To which I swiftly replied, "Indeed, *we* always do…"

You smiled then. You smiled with that subtle smile that always characterized you. I could never fully decipher whether you were really smiling or pretending to do so. At first, I thought you were amused by the coincidence that we both belonged to the same college, but that quickly changed to a suspicion that your grin was due to the grotesque bet of thirty-eight colleges in thirty-eight nights (the absurd pastime of one of those stupid brotherhoods, which consisted of sleeping with a different girl from each of the thirty-eight colleges on thirty-eight consecutive nights). But you lost, with me you lost (technically, at least). Now, I'm the one who smiles, remembering your desperate face —by the door of my room— where I made you wait just long enough for you to lose your bet and make love not on that evening but at dawn. That's how our world is, isn't it? A competitive place, where we always make sure that we are the conquerors and not the conquered.

As I remember you, I wish with all my strength that I could travel back in time to find you there again, in Port Meadow, surrounded by nature, by peace, by ourselves — by the ones we were, before we stopped being. I wonder whether if we were granted a second chance, we would still make the same fatal mistake: losing the magic. Perhaps, it was not really our fault, but the fault of love itself, and what love is made of: ethereal matter. Anyway, when I close my eyes, I can still imagine you there, surrounded by the hairy horses, by the woolly sheep, by the feathery geese, overflowing with a feverish drive to understand the world, empowered by our perennial youth, still virgins, so…

When I first saw you, my second assumption was that you would be studying something for nerds. Maybe electronics and heat dissipation, or perhaps quantum physics. I had just broken up with a boyfriend who drove me crazy with his eternal conversations about quantum physics and the stochastic models that, according to him, were the explanation for all the secrets of the universe, including love. Honestly, I had not the slightest intention of getting into another boring relationship with someone egocentric and monothematic. When you confessed that you were doing your Ph.D. on game theory and the refinement of John Nash's equilibrium, trust me: you were very close to being automatically eliminated. But you were saved—in extremis—when you strategically added, "Although I like to read Lord Byron. Sometimes." You made me laugh. You always lied so badly. But I found your transparent dishonesty somehow flattering.

I tested you: "What are your favorite verses?"

To which you replied, with full confidence and without a pinch of doubt, "The unpublished ones."

You were always such a tempting liar... The topic of my Ph.D. was about how different forms of colonialism introduced different institutional arrangements in the colonies, and how this subsequently influenced the economic and social development of the colonized countries. When I finished describing the subject of my doctoral dissertation, perhaps in more detail than you needed to hear, I realized how unbelievably boring I sounded, and felt obliged to add, "But I read Lord Byron, twice a day." You laughed, I laughed, and, with that foolish laughter that novice lovers use, we started walking like two fools in love.

We wandered the streets for hours, fearing that we might run out of them at some point. We walked along the cobbled Woodstock Road while the lampposts began to color a postcard-like twilight. In front of Green College, looking at the Radcliffe Observatory, you told me, passionately, how on one occasion you spent the whole night awake, contemplating the birth of a new blue star through the enormous telescope, and how that extraordinary experience also meant the birth of your new self. I didn't believe a word of that, although I appreciated the poetry of your voice and the lyricism of your knowing glances.

Then, we crossed through the alley of North Parade Avenue —always adorned with little colorful flags— and in front of the historic creperie, I told you that in that restaurant they served a cream-and-chocolate crepe with hazelnut liqueur that had been honored with my name, Gipani, in gratitude for the summer that I worked there as a waitress to pay for a trip to Pergamum that I had always dreamed of. You didn't believe me either, and you did well, because it wasn't true, but I felt the compelling need to add a fantastic story to all those fantasies of yours.

We arrived at Banbury Road, the street of the huge stone houses, and it was precisely there that you tenderly held me by the shoulder and I was assailed by the fleeting and intrepid thought of what it would feel like if you carried me in your arms (all these emotions were growing so fast inside me!). I actually would find out, years later, although in different circumstances than those I had imagined, when you carried me, wounded by crossfire during a demonstration against the government in the streets of Phnom Penh.

We crossed the university parks in the sunset as the last lovers were standing up from the grass after making quiet love, still with little twigs tangled in their hair and their lips bruised. We sat on the bench placed there in honor of J. R. R. Tolkien, and from there we watched the boats retreating gently, leaving behind a timid backwash and several bobbing swans along the way. The ocher tones began to crown that time of the year. It felt idyllic, and I never quite knew whether those blues resonating in the distance really came from the other side of the river or from the other side of our common sense.

As everything seemed too dream-like, somehow too intoxicating, I began to panic (and I believe you did too), perhaps because we both felt we were advancing too rapidly toward the edge of the abyss. We decided to move back to safety by talking about the most aseptic thing we could come up with (the weather, I think). And when we didn't know what else to say about that, we came back to the important topics: the economy, society, development... and then we returned to the fables of life and how they sometimes conspire, tricking us by making us believe magic hides around the next corner. One thing led to another, and we finally found ourselves discussing again the essential issue —the mystery of living— which we explored as we plunged back into the intricacies of the city.

We followed the trail of the scent of burning wood exhaled by the chimneys, which will always inevitably remind me of you. We walked through the alabaster passageways, surrounded by stone walls oozing centuries of history, until we came across the Sheldonian Theater, with its gargoyles and blazons of other times, and the old Bodleian Library, also with its testimonies of the past, and, finally, we stumbled across the Radcliffe Camera, where students congregated wearing a uniform of multicolored scarves. The old Raleigh bicycles reminded us of how things were in the past while we silently began to concoct how it could be (for us) in the future. By then, the evening had already conquered the city and, with that coming and going of short phrases, sidelong glances, and the occasional sigh of illusion, we surprised ourselves by seeking refuge from the cold in one of the historic pubs: the Eagle & Child.

It's funny how one experiences that certainty —that of falling in love— only a handful of times in life… It is, perhaps, one of the most ephemeral feelings the soul can feel. It doesn't last longer than a leaf takes to fall from a tree, but, as it falls (as we fall), the sensation is so wonderfully harmonic that one wants to experience it again and again. Yet the fatality of life makes it impossible, and the worst fatality of all is, perhaps, the desire to experience it again. Once the leaf touches the ground, it has fallen forever. Fortunately, though, that evening the leaf had not fallen, yet. So, we ordered two cappuccinos; you ordered a very hot one with skimmed milk and a cold croissant filled with cream, and I ordered my cappuccino with cream, cold milk, and a plain croissant. You still drank cow's milk then instead of almond milk, and the only intolerance you had was to death. The intolerance to lactose came years later, when we were already living in Washington, D.C., and by then we had become so intolerant to so many things that cow's milk was only a minor intolerance.

I remember that you always carried a pocket notebook to record random observations about some invisible world of yours that you always claimed existed for anyone willing to see it. You never stopped writing in that notebook, and even with the advent of modern mobile phones, you persevered in using that anachronistic tool. You had the amazing ability to take your notebook out naturally, without losing the thread of the conversation, almost without caring, and so naturally that it was difficult for the other to pose the question, "What the hell are you writing in there?"

It was not until the third time I saw you doing it that I could no longer resist the temptation, and I asked you, "Are you documenting something?"

To which you answered, soberly, "Yes, the future."

You were always so enigmatic and sincere. But, yes, indeed, that's what you were actually trying to do: predict the future. You and your eccentric experiments, which at that time led you to develop prediction models based on instinct. The idea was simple: you would write down your hunches to later check if they were fulfilled or not. I spent the whole afternoon insisting that you let me read your mysterious observations, and only after much obstinacy did I convince you to read me two. One was that I would order my coffee without sugar, although with double cream, and the other that I would insist on paying the bill. In both cases you were right, but for the wrong reason.

Your prediction that I would insist on paying the bill was based on the perception of my feminist side, which, although true, wasn't my ultimate motivation. I really wanted to pay the bill because, that way, you would have proposed having a second drink —something I desperately wanted. Your explanation of your first prediction was hilarious. According to you, I would order my coffee without sugar but with lots of cream, because —you wrote— I was "an ocean of contradictions." But you were wrong. I was always a fairly consistent person, and I think you transferred a description of yourself onto me. I was tempted to deny your description of me, but I liked your poetry so much that I ended up accepting it as valid, and, paraphrasing Walt Whitman, I said, "Do I contradict myself? Very well, then I contradict myself; I am large, I contain multitudes."

Your riskiest predictions weren't those two, but the one that years later I discovered while I was searching among your things, looking for traces of a crime you committed, in part, and I found your mysterious little notebook. Only then did I discover your most audacious prediction of that night: "I'm going to marry her." And then you added, "And our love will be eternal, until it stops being so."

In that cafe you said to me, "Tell me about yourself." And leaning back casually in your chair, you readied yourself for the naked confession I was not prepared to make. In a futile effort to protect my privacy, I jokingly said that I hold a British passport and that, therefore, I was not used to talking about myself, much less with a stranger. You showed yourself as Spanish again when, looking straight into my eyes, almost melting them, you said, "You're right: now we are still two strangers, but if we talk about ourselves, we stop being so, little by little."

In a fraction of a second, I realized that you were the chosen one, or that I was the chosen (I still don't know what the difference is), so I decided not to delay the inevitable anymore and jumped into the void, without any safety net whatsoever. For the first time in my life, I felt that love is a fragile bridge between two passions —

instinct and hope— across which one advances, intrepidly, but with the growing fear that one's vulnerability would not be reciprocated at the other end. At that moment, my instinct was to keep walking across that footbridge and journey into the unknown, so I added that a quarter of me is Burmese.

I gave you a bit of background history first, trying to bring the emotions down a bit, so I explained that my grandmother was Burmese and my grandfather was English. They met during the Second World War, when he was a prisoner in a Japanese concentration camp in Myanmar. Urmila, my grandmother, was forced to work in the service of the Japanese army as a nurse, although she wasn't one. In charge of bringing water to each cell, she met my grandfather, who remained captive there for almost two years. Each day, she would bring him two cups of water: one in the morning and one in the afternoon. They were not allowed to speak, touch, or make much eye contact. She brought him water and, in a way, also life, both physically at first and spiritually later.

My grandfather stoically resisted the first twelve months of captivity, but then his hopes to leave that camp alive began to fade and his soul began to languish. When my grandmother felt that he was dying of sadness, she made a gesture that probably saved his life. She began to smear her lips with butter, and before giving him a drink from the cup, she drank first so that the imprint of her lips would be left on the edge. The mere presence of a tenuous breath, the warmth of lips on the cold metal —that sign of love, in short— brought him back to life. When years later, already elderly, she was admitted to hospital in London and, feeling the breath of death, she entrusted herself to heaven, it was my grandfather who saved her from dying, with improvised poems that didn't rhyme under any criterion or metric but were so loaded with pure love that they helped prolong her life for an extra six months. He invested this time in composing a whole book of poems —unstructured and assonant— that helped him finally spit out all the feelings he had so carefully saved for himself during a lifetime of playing the perfect Englishman.

I proceeded with my unexpected revelations, which surprised even me. After several sips of my coffee, I jumped to tell you how that one quarter of my Asian soul was everything for me; how it had profoundly influenced my perception of the small and invisible things; how it shaped who I was, but also how the other three quarters of my tamed Western soul was in almost constant conflict with my overwhelming desire to live immersed in nothing but feelings, without caring about the palpable world, without having to feel guilty for losing a minute of the time carved out by modern life that leaves not a second for the life that really matters. I spilled myself in a myriad of confessions —something unprecedented for me. It paid its dividends: half a life with you (a pity that it couldn't be a whole life).

The pub's fireplace attracted distant glances from patrons while the mulled wine continued to enlighten the conversations of novice students, wise professors, and those other candid souls. By the time we left the pub, we had so much coffee in our bodies that we could have stayed awake for the rest of our lives. I lived in college accommodation, while you lived crowded in a shabby little room, beyond Summer Town, along with other students who, like you, left formalizing registration to the last moment and were accorded no place in paradise. Even though your final destination was far beyond mine, you insisted on accompanying me along the entire Banbury Road on the pretext that you would get on the first bus that passed through toward your abode. The number three bus passed, and you decided not to take it, arguing that it wouldn't be responsible or courteous to abandon me to my own fortune with that rabid dog that had been reported loose by the local authorities. Later, the number two bus arrived, and you let it go, pretending to chase a squirrel behind the cypress hedge, although cocking my ear, I could hear the whisper of your glorious urine. The number three bus came again, and this time your excuse was that a guy inside the bus had given you a dirty look and that you didn't want problems that night. Finally, even your roommate passed in his car and shouted at you from the other side of the street, offering you a ride, and you yelled back that you had no clue who the hell he was, to which he replied by showing you his middle finger (and reminding you that you were late on paying the rent, by the way).

"I'm not going to sleep with you tonight," I told you.

"Really?" you replied, surprised, while you turned to check if your roommate was still there waiting for you.

Then, you pretended that none of that had happened and you returned to the conversation rather innocently. When we finally reached my college —already at my doorstep— I slid the key into the lock and, when you assumed that in a matter of seconds you would be lying on my bed, I asked, "What time is it?"

"Like midnight," you replied, without even looking at your watch.

"What time is it, exactly?" I insisted.

You looked at your watch, annoyed.

"Twelve minutes to twelve," you answered.

"We must wait," I said.

"For what?"

"We must wait," I said, providing no further reasons.

Your face spoke volumes. I literally had to bite my tongue to keep from bursting into tears of laughter.

"Is it because your roommate is in?" you asked.

"I live alone," I bluntly replied. "We must wait."

You frowned and accepted that your destiny (and your sex life) was at my mercy and that the most sensible thing to do was to behave. And there we remained, looking at each other like two fools in the dim light of the corridor, without much else to say. Two minutes later, which must have seemed like twenty to you, you asked again, "Are we ready?"

"No. We must wait," I replied again.

I remember you pulling a face reminiscent of desperate children queuing for their cotton candy clouds at the funfair.

"It's because your room is messy, and you left all your underwear spread around, right?" you asked. "But I don't care, I promise I don't! Besides, waiting here outside in this damn cold, the clothes aren't going to sort themselves out, you know...," you said, comically.

"We must wait," I replied, rejoicing, I must confess, for the power granted by the moment.

The queue for cotton candy became infinite.

"What time is it?" I asked again.

"It's midnight," you replied, hopeless.

"Exactly midnight?"

"Three minutes to midnight," you replied.

"Then you must keep waiting," I said.

Bored and desperate, you began to play with the zipper of your jacket, raising and lowering it, until it broke, and you started trying to fix it, squinting under a light bulb that shed as much light as a match. I would give almost anything to return to that moment, so childish, so innocent, so carefree: essential ingredients for the spring of love.

"What time is it?" I asked again.

"I don't know... don't you see I'm busy...," you responded, absorbed with your new entertainment.

"Do you want to play children's or adults' games...?" I asked.

"Past midnight!" you replied swiftly.

"Let's go inside then."

Lying on the bed, you placed your warm hand on my smooth belly, and my body became a dune. You wandered unrestrained underneath my blouse to the forbidden confines of my hips; ruffling hairs, raising winds, describing circles of love around a bellybutton transformed into an oasis. A balmy mist spread across us, filling the spaces not yet occupied by you, the shadows not yet cleared by me. You built an invisible gangway bridging the abyss that separated my prudence from my own desire, and you helped me cross it by sliding your wise fingers across my body, recognizing the skin of the new woman, examining blindly the flesh that you felt was unconquered.

You went on and on, tempting my instincts —tempted by your own as well— going through sandstone valleys and sandy hills, until you stumbled across my aura, and, here, you moistened your thumb and forefinger and provoked the still-flaccid breast, which quickly acquired the turgidity of succulent plants. And from that cardinal point (which you called your Milky Way) you camped, furtively, taking perhaps too much liberty for a first encounter, but to which I responded with the sigh of a grateful woman that you rightly interpreted as a welcoming sign. Now you know about my precocity and all its mysteries, but you didn't yet at that point, and I rejoiced in contemplating your expression of surprise when you noticed my ecstasy, which, although brief and well-contained, sounded like glorious music.

And then you shifted, fairly intrepidly, aiming for my other hill, where you also found yourself welcomed. You strived at pleasing me, and then you said, "The last thing I want is that they get jealous of each other." After a while there, since you couldn't unleash the thunderstorms that you were expecting to, you started kissing me softly all along my neck, and a new intimate mystery was then revealed to you. But when you tried to again cut across my belly —now more confidently— and in the unequivocal direction, toward the forbidden forest, I stopped you, not because I didn't desire you, but to be desired even more. At that point the hunter became the prey, and, with the precise moves of an agile gazelle, I switched positions, lying down on top of you. I took off my blouse and, just as I was about to unclasp my bra, you said, "Don't! To release them is my duty…"

You put your hand on my back and, in a skillful finger snap, my bra fell, irrecoverable. I instantly noticed how that joyful gesture of liberation extended your love for me by a few extra centimeters. You looked at me like the prey you were and said, "What do we do now with the tiger we just hunted?"

"Enjoy it," I replied.

I don't think you expected such an esoteric response from someone you judged (good and bad) as analytical. With time you understood that a woman dressed in clothes is one thing, but a woman dressed in skin is quite another.

I caressed your hair, letting the strands run between my fingers, and then tugged a lock to announce that I too could be wild in the forest of the tender bed. I recounted the fact that we had not yet kissed, and I remembered the saying that kisses are like the dust on the wings of butterflies, which is lost by abuse until the wings become useless —and the kisses no longer make you fly. And as I sensed that I would want to fly much further with you than that first evening, I proposed that we not kiss then, but later, and then that "later" was delayed until it became a kiss that never arrived. What began as a game of resisting the temptation to kiss later became a competition to see who succumbed to the desire for that first kiss. The truth is that three months after that first night, and already as a formal couple, we still had not kissed for various reasons, none of them true. It was not until that dinner at Gee's — where we spent all our savings with a starter, entree, and dessert at one of the most exclusive restaurants on Banbury Road— that we confessed the inevitable: we were scared to death. With more detours than allowed for in my Anglo-Saxon culture and certainly with more metaphors than allowed in any culture, you told me that you were horrified at the thought of ending up as one of those elderly couples who sit in the park and don't speak because they have already said everything. They don't look at each other because they've already seen everything, nor do they touch each other because they've already touched everything. I, with fewer words, confessed the same thing. "Everything is ephemeral," I told you.

But in our erotic moments, we forgot those considerations, and everything was madness and spontaneity. I remember how you, unexpectedly, jumped out of bed and went out through the huge window that overlooked the college pond so that, in your own words, we could get to know the newly arrived geese better. The breath of fresh grass spread throughout the room, and the vapors of the Cherwell River floated up to us as if inviting us to enjoy one of those mystical moments that remind one that life is today. The boats floated serenely on the pond, wrapped in a mystical mist, and under the majestic oak a few patches of stony snow gave off a magical fluorescence. The city was peacefully asleep on the other side of that darkness, and the dim glow of the tungsten lights bathed everything in a sepia tint. It looked like one of those fancy postcards you buy for ten cents, and the most wonderful thing is that that fantasy of others was indeed our reality.

I wonder now what became of those geese who, in fact, were newcomers and who celebrated the move by beating their broad wings against the water. I wonder if in their global migrations they will have seen us again on some of our missions in Africa, or maybe when we lived in Cambodia. Or maybe in Arlington Pond, when we were already residing in Washington, where we used to go on Sundays after couples' therapy, often returning separately after having argued once again. Luckily, on that first night in Oxford, we still allowed ourselves to shudder with the beating of those geese wings; we still found in the cold the call of awakened nature, instead of thinking without saying, "You want to close the damn window—I'm freezing!" We still heard in the hiss of the wind a hymn to freedom.

Still framed in the window of my room, and exhibiting your nakedness so naturally, you let yourself go into a miraculous trance, absorbing all the essence of nature that you managed to retain in your deep inspiration. Then you turned to me again, with the unequivocal intention of returning to bed. I was the one who made a gesture unknown to myself. Instinctively, I would almost say lasciviously, I let the sheet slip to the floor and exposed myself, completely naked, on the bed, as in a portrait by Matisse. I did it because a clothed word doesn't say anything, but a naked look says it all; I did it because I wanted you to observe me and be able to verify what you really felt for me. Your reaction was unequivocal: you didn't develop an erection immediately. Instead, your eyes became wet, and then I gained the irrefutable certainty that what was about to happen was a lesson of love.

# CHAPTER TWO

## ONE MORE DAY AT THE WORLD BANK

It was 6:50 a.m. in Washington, D.C. More than twenty years had elapsed since that first magical evening in Oxford. I'm still unsure of what exactly happened between that mystical first walk and the subsequent steps that led to a dawn deprived of almost all colors. I woke up alone, as usual. No longer absorbed by love, I was now absorbed in my career.

While in Washington, I used to wake up exactly ten minutes before seven to listen to the 7:10 news, capturing ten more minutes of pleasurable "me time" until 7:20. In D.C., life is measured in fractions of time, and anything beyond that measure of time is simply considered excessive. The truth is that I never really liked listening to the news in the morning because of the bitterness it brings hearing about the misfortunes of the planet Earth. However, I just couldn't afford to be ambushed in the office in a conversation concerning a subject about which I was utterly clueless. To be asked, with false paternalism, by a colleague, "But aren't you aware of…?" was simply devastating.

So, during those ten glorious minutes, my mind was divided between my conscious side, which tried to avidly absorb facts and statistics, and my subconscious, which struggled to enjoy the furtive aroma of the organic coffee, the warmth of the cup between my hands, trying to reconnect with the little habits of the past that had now become almost illegal indulgences. But, of course, the shrill background noise of some ambulance or the persistent hooting of the traffic would remind me that we live in a modern world where we have to live in the present tense —the present imposed by others, of course— and where dedicating time to the small things is simply unacceptable.

By 7:40, I would be on my way to the office. I liked to walk there. Almost every day I would cover on foot the brief twenty minutes that separated my home from the MC building at the World Bank. Those twenty minutes were probably my only daily opportunity to breathe the unfiltered air inside that wonderful city of glass that is the headquarters of the Bank. Once in the street, I followed an almost martial path. I would go down two blocks along Nineteenth Street until I reached the coffee shop on the corner, where I would buy one of those recycled cardboard cups with a non-recycled plastic lid of fair-trade coffee with artificial sweetener. After having the first coffee at home, drinking a second cup within a few minutes was completely redundant, but in the same way it was inconceivable to enter through that enormous door of the Bank without carrying one of those coffees and being like everyone else. It was simply something that ought to be done.

My walking routine was prodigiously planned. It encompassed what I used to call the rule of the twin lights. In the days when I felt inspired and of pure heart —and still like a believer in development— I would wait until the precise moment when the first traffic light went from red to green, and then I walked slowly to synchronize my pace with the second traffic light, arriving there just as it was turning red. The reason was non-intuitive: a beggar used to beg down at that second traffic light. His name was Jack (I think). He was a black man in his fifties (I presume), who always wore several layers of colorful sweaters, under which he placed dozens of paper balls to deal with the inclemency of the cold nights. His fear of the cold was such that even in the height of summer he would still wear all those layers of clothing. To fear the cold! Such a primitive instinct, understandable perhaps in prehistoric humans living in caves, but simply inexplicable among humans living a few hundred meters away from the White House. However, Jack played the saxophone as if he had not known the meaning of sadness in his entire life, although he was quite likely made of sadness. He spoke to me only once, and only one sentence, in the seven years that I stumbled upon him almost daily, but I have tried to imagine his distant life countless times. Surely, he did the same with me as well, and, most probably, we had something in common: our past was more musical than our present. I used to throw a dollar into his hat, for which he always thanked me by playing a crazy note with his worn-out sax.

That was on the days when I felt happy. On those when I was skeptical about most things —even about life itself— at the first traffic light, I chose to pause until the light would turn green, just to reach the second traffic light as it turned green too (without having to stop), thus avoiding the beggar. I would, nevertheless, excuse myself by pointing to the traffic light to make him understand that I was in a rush, presumably due to some urgent meeting. I was making excuses to a man who probably knew little about meetings, let alone the notion of being late, except to his own life, perhaps. Even so, the beggar would play a special note for me, although, this time, it would be a melancholic flat, which I always interpreted as of his own sadness, until, one day, he broke his silence and added to his sad note, "I hope you can be yourself tomorrow." Suddenly, I found myself crying; I cried because I understood that he felt sorry for me (and not the other way around). How devastating that can be… Fortunately, though, within just a few meters I reached my oasis of the World Bank building, flanked by the White House on the left and the International Monetary Fund on the right, where I was the practice manager for the Health Sector of Southeast Asia and the Pacific. I was in the safe box.

I still remember the first time I entered the main building of the World Bank, after having worked for many years for other smaller development organizations in Senegal and Tanzania. When I found myself in the middle of the atrium —a beautiful glass internal plaza— I was left open-mouthed, looking up at that futuristic inner city. While I stood totally mesmerized by it, someone approached me from behind and said, "Do you feel the cold?" I didn't understand at that precise moment what he meant by that. Years later, just after leaving a high-profile meeting, one of those in which one feels pleased to have used all the usual jargon without really saying much, I was the one who approached that same person, who by then was one of the regional vice presidents. I said, "I'm freezing to death." His reply was laced with irony:

"Congratulations, you just climbed to the top of the mountain."

And so it is: the career ladder often very much feels like climbing a mountain. You normally start working from the base, which, in the case of the development sector, usually translates as working for an NGO, for example. Here, still at the bottom, you can feel the human warmth, enjoy the interaction with people made of flesh and blood. You know their names and they know yours, you help them (or at least you assume so), you shake their hands, you embrace them; you eat their food, you're glad of their fortunes and cry at their misfortunes; you can touch, see, and even smell their everyday problems. But the paradox is that you're so close to them that you can't always discern the ultimate solution. You're young at the time. Life is beautiful, and it feels infinite.

However, one day frustration knocks on your door, and you feel that what you do has such a limited impact that it may not even be worth it. Then, in a genuine attempt to gain a better perspective, to find the universal solution to all evils that afflict the world, to be able to have a greater impact, you finally decide to start climbing that mountain of career progression. You aren't so young by then, and the bills become less manageable. Halfway through the ascension, you get, effectively, a better view. You can now see entire neighborhoods, towns, and even other distant hills. The trade-off, though, is that people seen from this height are no longer people but rather silhouettes and living shadows. You now have to guess which problems torment them daily, since not even the echoes make it up there.

Even so, life is good at that higher altitude. The air is cleaner, and the prospects are good. But, after a while, you get up again one morning, supposedly motivated by giving yourself to the cause fully, and ultimately decide to complete the ascension. You ask yourself, perhaps guided by a sense of purpose (maybe mixed with some ego as well), whether the view will not be even better from the very top, and, consequently, if the impact of your work wouldn't be even greater too. You then equip yourself with icy picks and crampons, with ropes and tons of faith, and launch the final assault to the summit.

In my case, reaching the top was reaching the World Bank. At the World Bank, the perspective is, by definition, global; you no longer work with poor people, but with poor countries and their respective governments (which are sometimes not so poor); you no longer visit a bunch of dispersed little rundown houses but a handful of much larger ones —called ministries. The quality of the work is incomparable, the professionalism of your colleagues is unbeatable, and the satisfaction enormous. The power to do good appears almost unlimited, and you feel all-powerful and immortal. What more could you ask for, up there on the mountain? The answer is nothing. The single drawback, however, is that when one day you decide to look out onto the balcony of the world, you're so high up that you can see almost nothing… just ice. No cities or houses, much less people; ice, just ice, and, then, you suddenly experience extreme cold: that of solitude.

As a manager, my schedule for the day was tight. First, I had a working breakfast with the practice manager for governance in the East African Region, then other minor meetings, followed by a lunch with the UNICEF representative for Vietnam. After that, a ton of piled-up e-mails. But the three key milestones of the day were a decision meeting regarding the new financing cycle for Cambodia (a country to which I had to travel days later), a review meeting to assess progress made in the analytical portfolio of Myanmar and, undoubtedly the most important of all, the preparatory meeting to climb Everest, for the project named *ICE* (I Climbed Everest).

ICE initially consisted of fundraising for the construction of a school in Mozambique. However, the challenge evolved into a bike ride between Bethesda and Arlington, sponsored by a private company that would support the initiative financially in exchange for brand exposure, and later escalated into a cycling competition along the road between Washington, D.C., and New York, which would be covered by local TV stations. Then the idea further expanded to cover the hundreds of miles stretching between the East and West Coasts. But this plan would involve the participation of one of the regional vice presidents who the founding group disliked. Consequently, the group finally decided to take the challenge to the next level: to climb to the third base camp on Everest. This would guarantee the automatic withdrawal of the undesirable vice president because it was well known that he suffered from vertigo.

To make the challenge even more fun (or rather more competitive and in line with the spirit of the Bank), it was suggested to create two teams: one composed of colleagues from the human development sector (health, education, and social protection), and another of colleagues from the macroeconomics department. When I was approached to participate in this mad expedition, I responded, without much thought, "Yes!" I believe I must have become carried away by the itch to escape routine. Later, however, when I saw your name on the list of participants from the macroeconomists' team, I must admit that I oscillated between an irrational yes and a cautious no, until I ultimately decided to go, perhaps more driven by pride than common sense.

"Why could we not share this activity?" I asked myself. We were adults, and, after all, a fair amount of time had already elapsed since our separation, which would supposedly have cooled our emotions. In addition, the teams would depart at different times, so the risk of coinciding for longer than necessary was minimal. I tried to persuade myself that I had already overcome the toughest phase of our separation. (A huge lie, as a matter of fact: how could anyone ever overcome the loss of the love of your life?) There was evidence that we were over it. On several occasions, we had seen each other in the so-called spring meetings in Washington, when you came to headquarters from your new country office in Nicaragua. We were never involved in any major, regrettable incidents, with the exception, perhaps, of that agitated verbal battle between us that took place in public —in the context of the new reforms introduced by our recently appointed president. But I choose to believe that even that had been strictly professional and uncontaminated by any sentimental unsettled background emotion (perhaps another subconscious lie). I still remember your last phrase as you tightly held the microphone: "There are reforms that are sometimes painful, but also necessary." To which I replied, also microphone in hand, "Were things not better in the old days?"

At 9.00 am Washington, D.C., time, the videoconference for the decision meeting on the new financing proposal for the health sector in Cambodia began. I, as the practice manager for health, was responsible for facilitating the conversation from headquarters. I was accompanied by the evaluators, who had sent comments on the document (the PAD —Project Appraisal Document), which described the various areas to be financed. From the Bangkok office —the regional headquarters covering Cambodia— the director, Bram Fischer, an Austrian well known for his appetite for excessive perfectionism, would act as chair, and from the Phnom Penh office, the health team, led by Tim Potter, would connect to defend the proposal.

The proposal was for an US$80 million loan to the Ministry of Health, to be disbursed using an innovative financing instrument called Payment for Results (P4R) that the World Bank had been experimenting with recently. The World Bank, tired of decades of financing projects and making loans that often resulted in nothing, was beginning to implement this new system that involved segmenting loans and disbursing amounts to local governments as the mutually agreed goals were reached. The program that was intended to be financed was a package of interventions that the Cambodian government was preparing to launch to reduce the high rate of infant and maternal mortality, and the high rates of malnutrition.

The loan was divided into ten areas called DLIs, or Disbursement Linked Indicators, each with objectives the government committed to achieve over the next five years, receiving the funds from the loan as goals were reached. Priority areas the Ministry of Health was advised to emphasize included, for example, increasing the vaccination coverage among children and the percentage of births attended by specialized personnel in health facilities. Other recommendations involved policy reforms. For example, previous studies carried out by the World Bank had identified unequal budget distribution among the provinces that didn't correspond to real needs. Thus, another DLI consisted of rewarding the government for correcting these inequities.

The purpose of the decision meeting was to assess the quality and adequacy of the proposal and approve the next steps: proceeding with final negotiation with Cambodia's Ministry of Economy and Finance before the approval by the Bank's Board of Directors in Washington. This long and complex process normally takes more than a year to complete.

"Good morning in D.C., good evening in Asia," said Bram through the huge screen in the video conference room. "It's 8 p.m. here in Bangkok, and this meeting stands between a long workday and a cocktail invitation at the Korean Embassy that I must attend, so let's be efficient with time, please. If there is no objection to the proposed agenda, I would suggest that we begin by looking at the comments made by the reviewers in the review matrix, OK?"

Everyone nodded on their respective screens, although I felt compelled to make a remark, mainly to clarify that, although he was the regional director, I was the practice manager of the entire Southeast Asia and Pacific region: "OK, Bram," I said, "but I'd like to add to the agenda a discussion around best strategies to incorporate the additional financing the Australians seem determined to channel through us in this project."

"Are you referring to the twenty million dollars the kangaroos want to recycle into vaccines?" he asked sarcastically. "OK, let's discuss that at the end, although with that new incoming government in Melbourne, which is somewhat less philanthropic than the previous one, we will see if that contribution eventually materializes. Anything else to be included in the agenda?" he asked.

"Yes," replied the team leader in Cambodia. "I would like to also discuss the legitimacy of negotiating this loan with the newly formed government after those very contested last elections, whose results are still not accepted by the opposition party."

Bram fired his first accurate dart: "We work with whichever government has been elected to Parliament, without contemplating its political tendency, and without judging if it is to our liking or not. Our client is the local government, not their ideology, and our mission is not to support the government itself but to catalyze the development of the country by providing specific support to its government. And yes, in exceptional circumstances we may choose to freeze our lending operations, in extreme cases of poor governance, for example, but we must accept that our clients' gardens contain more thorns than roses."

"Well," Bram continued "if there is no more to add, let's proceed with the comments from the review matrix. The first one is about the verification of progress made in each of the result indicators that will trigger our disbursements. According to the reviewer, there does not seem to be enough detail in the document on how this will be done. Does anyone want to answer this question?"

Tim took the floor as team leader: "The verification of the results will be carried out through an independent validation agency of the government. In some cases, the World Bank will also conduct random field surveys to compare them with official data."

"OK," the director replied. "The second point deals with indicator number three, whose objective is to increase health personnel in rural areas, who are currently concentrated in urban areas where they are less needed. The reviewer asks what measures will be implemented to not only increase the number of health personnel but also the quality of the services provided."

I decided to take the lead on this occasion. "A pertinent comment, Bram," I replied. "DLI number three is intimately connected with indicators from DLIs four and five. Thus, DLI four promotes enhanced training of health personnel by, for example, rewarding the government monetarily for reviewing the curriculum currently applied in the Faculty of Medicine or promoting a more transparent and meritocratic student enrolment system. On the other hand, DLI five promotes the implementation of a rewards system via small performance-based bonuses for health personnel, linked to the achievement of established objectives and to patient satisfaction, which will be measured through social audits."

"That's all very well," replied Bram. "However, as I see in the document that describes the program... on page... thirty-eight, I think... Yes, here it is. Only thirty-five percent of patients seem to use public health services, while the other two thirds use private services or even the informal market, which I believe means dubious vendors dispatching multicolored pills in the streets. Therefore, what guarantees do we have that after all this investment on the supply side, user demand will actually increase?"

"That is correct," Tim swiftly replied. "It's an apparent paradox that the majority of the population choose to be treated in small private centers by healers, or even to buy medicines directly at the market, when the cost of doing so is generally higher and the quality of care is not necessarily of higher quality than that in public centers. There's a complex relationship between several parameters. On the one hand, if we look at the geographical mapping we carried out last year, it can be clearly seen that the distance to public health units is usually greater, and this means that there are many practitioners out there who, even when they lack the proper training, turn out to be more convenient for the patient who cannot afford covering the cost of transport to more distant public health centers."

"And improving the quality of the public health services will shorten that very same distance?" Bram asked, incisively.

I came to Tim's rescue: "Bram, this is indeed a relevant observation, but it's worth contemplating several aspects in an integrated way. The first is that DLI nine encourages the government to also introduce a transport subsidy for the poorest families, who, by the way, are beneficiaries of the free health care scheme. In this way, we're aiming to encourage users to go to the public health facilities, not only in the case of illness but also for vaccinations, nutrition monitoring, and antenatal visits.

"At the same time, the theory is that even those patients who'll still have to pay for their transportation will be more likely to go to public health services if they perceive that the quality of care is optimal. Finally, the quality improvement program not only includes increasing the knowledge of health personnel, or providing better instruments for diagnosis, but also additional training to improve the quality of engagement with the patient, like the amount of time spent or a more respectful interaction.

"Recent analytical studies clearly show that the quality of health services in the private sector is not necessarily superior to that of the public sector; rather, the main difference lies in the type of engagement with the patient."

Bram, with his unfortunate Austrian sense of humor, replied, "Maybe they should offer candies at the reception, as in the hospital in Vienna where they treat my prostate?" Some giggles came through the mics to please the director.

"OK, OK... I'm moderately persuaded by this argument," Bram replied, "but let's move on to the next point, because the Koreans are waiting for me to have dinner. DLI one: economic incentives for the Ministry of Economy and Finance to allocate a larger percentage of its internal budget for health expenditures. Interesting concept... If I understand it right, here we are paying the government to pay for its own health. Is that not something this government should do anyway without any further incentive?"

Bram, of course, knew the answer to his own question, but sometimes he liked to devote himself to rhetoric, setting aside the pragmatism everyone embraces so passionately at the Bank. I took the lead again: "I agree, Bram. We all know about the negative externalities of development aid. The more money we inject from outside, the less money is allocated from inside, from the state budget, leading to a substitution phenomenon and a zero-sum effect. With this DLI, we're trying to correct this negative effect and push the government to continue investing in the health sector with its own internal funds."

"I partially agree," Bram replied. "External aid does sometimes generate dependency; it is a catch twenty-two, I imagine. But let's not get too dramatic... Returning to this DLI, what you propose here seems sensible, and I want to congratulate the team for that. However, we must also be realistic: this government does not currently have the ability to mobilize much more domestic funding toward health. So, my question is, how can we teach the fisherman how to fish?"

Tim rushed to address this question: "Technical assistance. We plan to support the government in the preparation of a solid health financing strategy based on three fundamental pillars: mobilization of internal resources, improvements in efficiencies, and private sector engagement."

"Details, details, please...," interrupted Bram.

Tim took a breath. "We propose, for example, to conduct some analytical studies to see how the increase in tobacco taxation, from a tax rate currently very low compared to the rest of Southeast Asia, could generate more state revenue while at the same time reducing tobacco consumption."

"A word of caution here," interrupted Bram. "I do not want us to repeat the same mistake we made in the past in other countries, where the recommendation was to increase tobacco taxes by too small an order of magnitude, and what ultimately happened was that consumption did not decrease, and, in addition, the increase in the price of the pack of tobacco meant that the upper classes continued smoking regardless, while the lower classes suffered economically from the additional expense. So, let's make sure we provide the right advice so that this tax becomes a progressive one and does not affect the poor."

"Completely agreed," Tim replied.

"And what about the other reform proposals?" Bram asked.

Tim replied again: "In terms of the efficiency agenda, we have much room for improvement. We've estimated that up to forty percent of the resources is wasted due to inefficient allocation."

"Like for example…?" Bram asked.

Tim replied: "Procurement of pharmaceuticals. Currently, the government is paying between two and three times above the international benchmarking price. In addition, the supply mechanisms to the health units—"

"Wait a moment, wait a moment…" interrupted Bram. "Just to make sure we are all on the same page. Behind closed doors, and now that the ministry is not present in the conversation, we are all clear why the government is paying up to three times more for that, right? Are all of those present in this meeting aware of the existence of — allegedly, of course— fictitious companies affiliated with the government itself, and at the highest level, that supply those very same pharmaceuticals? Therefore, I would not call this a case of inefficiency, but an act of flagrant corruption. In front of the government, of course, we will use the euphemism *improvements in governance*, for example. But we all must know that this reform will by no means be accepted by the political establishment. That said, I completely agree that we must not continue turning a blind eye to this issue, which costs the Cambodian public treasury a whopping eighty million dollars a year, which is incidentally, more than we intend to finance through this loan. I propose being strategic about when to put this issue on the table, and I think the best timing will be in the context of the general budget support negotiations. We will make it clear then that, in order to continue contributing with our support, we must see gestures of goodwill first when it comes to reducing these... 'inefficiencies.'"

Bram was definitely one of the most irritating directors I had ever met, but also one of the best strategists in political economy.

Tim continued: "Thanks. Indeed, data from the latest surveys indicate substantial delays in the supply of medicines to health centers—"

"That we already know," interrupted Bram, "but what's the proposal?"

"To outsource this to the private sector, which tends to be far more efficient in the supply chain."

Bram began to rub his goatee, which was once blonde but now gray.

"Interesting... Something is for sure," said Bram. "I have never seen a cold beer not reaching any corner of even the most rural areas."

"Precisely!" exclaimed Tim.

"I also agree," I added. But I expressed reservations in this regard related to the optics from which this type of reform proposals could be seen.

"Meaning what?" Bram asked.

"Everyone at the Bank knows we're no longer the same neoliberal institution of the eighties. However, there are still institutions out there that strive to place us on that extreme, so they can position themselves on the more progressive side of the spectrum, which seems to please their audience more. In short, I'm slightly concerned about whether proposals such as introducing the private sector into state-core functions, like health, may not be misinterpreted as an attempt to privatize the health sector in Cambodia."

Bram looked serious.

"I see where your concern comes from, although I do not share the view that this should by any means influence the way we do things," said Bram. "We must move past the preoccupation with how others will perceive us. We simply cannot get along with everyone. This is not a birthday party. Our mission here is to advise each country of what we think is most convenient for their context. So, let's leave it up to the 'man in the sky' to judge us all on the on the Day of Judgment."

And with this biblical phrase and other even more solemn comments, the meeting went on until Bram noticed that his dinner with the Koreans was imminent, and that was the salvation for all, because as good a shepherd as he was, he also liked the sound of his own voice. I agreed with Tim to follow up on some of the discussions face to face since I had planned a mission to Cambodia in just a few weeks to work with the rest of the team on the more detailed development of the new health financing project. I had great hopes of that imminent trip to Cambodia, and I must admit that the ultimate reasons weren't strictly professional. I would also take advantage of that work mission to take a few days off after more than a year without having had a single day of vacation. I thought to visit again the most magical corners of the country, that is, the corners where you and I made love.

My afternoon meeting, the planning for the ascent of Everest, was undoubtedly the most frightening of all. Climbing that snow-covered mountain was certainly an intimidating thought, but the descent through my inner ice galleries was simply terrifying. I wasn't ready to see you again, yet I was far less ready to never see you again. I entered the videoconference room when the meeting had already begun. About ten of the sixteen participants were present in the room, while the rest were connected by video or audio from their respective country offices around the world.

When I arrived, the conversation revolved around what kind of crampons were optimal for the predicted weather conditions. In any group dynamic, there is always someone who feels superior to the rest, but, as the saying goes, in the land of the blind, the one-eyed man is king. On this occasion, all somehow felt like the king, and were giving each other all sorts of colorful advice. Fortunately, though, this mad adventure was a controlled one, because each of the two teams would be accompanied by two climbing experts accustomed to those alpine pantomimes for business groups with high purchasing power.

All the logistical aspects had carefully been contemplated by a professional company, and the only thing we had to do on our part was to enjoy the delusion that we were going to put our lives at risk as Sir Edmund Hillary did in his day. Even so, both teams had worked hard to organize numerous weekend training outings through the forests of Maryland, to enroll in expensive gyms in Washington, D.C., to purchase the very best sportswear online, to read books on Tibetan meditation, and to follow all sorts of diets designed for elite athletes. We had even become used to setting the air conditioning in the office to the coldest possible level to acclimatize to extreme temperatures.

The conversation about crampons went on and on, and at some point, it became like bees buzzing in my ear. Meanwhile, oblivious to everything and everyone, I remained silent in my corner, with my heart beating out of control, feeling the almost suffocating weight of your invisible presence. Unconsciously, perhaps, I chose the least visible place in the room, and I entrenched myself there, safe from your gaze through the camera. Out of the corner of my eye, though, I constantly looked at the small screen at the bottom labeled *Nicaragua* (your country office). Fortunately for my heart, your screen was minimized and the light was behind you, so I could barely see your silhouette. I chose to believe that you went for the backlight for the same reasons I placed myself in the shadow, that you chose not to ask any questions for the same reasons I remained silent, and that you didn't take your name off the list for this nonsensical adventure for the same reasons I didn't. Even though I wasn't fully aware of my own motives, in the same way that you probably weren't aware of yours…. Even when we both were probably guessing the other's motivations…

Deeply immersed in my silence, I concentrated on worshiping your silhouette. I noticed you squeezing half a lemon into a glass of water, and I couldn't suppress a smile when I saw that you still had that old habit of consuming half a lemon a day, under the pretext that it was good for the heart. You always claimed that this scientific knowledge came from one of your mother's lullabies: "*...unas gotitas de limón, para que funcione bien tu corazón...*" (a few lemon drops, so that the heart can go on). I concocted the idea that you were squeezing that lemon right at that moment for my own benefit. Driven by that assumption, I decided to reciprocate. I gathered my hair on top of my head and fastened it with a yellow pencil. I hadn't done this in years. I remembered when you used to approach me from behind and, looking at that seashell shape made of hair, you would place your ear over it to hear what you claimed were the sea sounds of my thoughts. You would then invent a magical story that often made me laugh. And so many times we would end up rolling around on the floor, making love.

After playing with my hair, I thought your silhouette responded to me. I believed you were playing with a piece of paper, shaping a cone that vaguely resembled a shell. I spent several minutes looking closely at the little screen, trying to imagine that you were really doing that: sending me a signal. But to my dismay, you finally wrapped the half-squeezed lemon in the paper and threw it in the trash. I felt like an idiot. I ripped the pencil out of my hair, letting my unkempt tresses fall over my face. I felt so ridiculous that I was about to get up and leave the room. But then I noticed a flash of silver on your wrist, and my curiosity returned. Maybe it was the bracelet engraved with that phrase of ours that I gave you on our trip to Monte Albán in Mexico and that you promised to *always* carry (although it was eventually whenever you remembered*).* Beautiful memories came to mind. One of them was how we spent days debating two job offers you had simultaneously received: a poorly paid job but a perfect fit for your heart, versus a well-paid job you would have hated. You chose with the heart (youth is such a divine treasure).

Still, in that videoconference room, we carried on playing a silent game of indecipherable signs, playing Chinese shadow puppets and other ambiguous games. We kept asking ourselves about the divine designs, questioning whether they are truly divine or just subconsciously chosen, and whether with a little more effort, with a little less pride, we would both have managed to redirect our relationship toward a happier ending. Meanwhile, oblivious to all our deeper thinking, and after almost two hours in that room, the two "wise men" of the group continued to monopolize the conversation about the crampons of choice. I wondered what miracle would have to happen for us to descend from that mountain still good friends.

At the end of the meeting, I urgently needed to reconnect with the umbilical cord of my past life, so I did what I always did in cases of extreme necessity: I visited my armored heart. Years back, anguished with the thought of losing my nomadic life and any of the precious treasures that constitute my past, I decided to keep some of them in the safe of a commercial bank. It was one of my best kept secrets. One of the few people to whom I revealed it called me "the woman with a heart locked in a safe deposit box." I always wonder to what extent that definition was just a metaphor.

For me, that aseptic room made of steel represented the place of all places, the most magical place of all. At the center of that hive-like room lined with thousands of safe deposit boxes was a table on which the guard would deposit my coffer before leaving me alone, surrounded only by silence and memories. Whenever I opened that box, I instantly traveled back in time to childhood, to that cotton-wrapped infancy of pure white, to that childhood of simple songs and easy words, to that childhood when you believe that the best is yet to come (only to later discover that the best has already passed).

I opened the box to take out all the objects one by one, as always, in a fixed order. First my father's watch, my mother's, and one of mine that she bought for me during the last shopping trip we went on together, for Christmas. The hands of my parents' watches mark the exact time when they said farewell to me; those of my watch, however, continue turning and turning. Yet I've always had the strange sensation that their watches seem to have more time left than mine.

I dug inside the coffer to find a golden pendant that belonged to my mother—tree shaped and embedded with little gems. I then pulled out a deck of old photographs. The first one, turned to sepia, is of my parents in Egypt, working as volunteers in a rural area. My father wears an ivory-color fedora hat and a meticulous tie —very British— while my mother wears a long dress made of cotton and timeless beauty. Whenever I admire that photograph, I always ask myself the same question: did they feel cold too? That unavoidable impulse to idealize the old days... For all I know it is just a bucolic disease (to be avoided at all costs), yet I often conclude that those times were more magical and that those sepia images were indeed sepia-colored and not tainted by nostalgia.

Before browsing through more of the photos, I found my mother's perfume. It's a small bottle of Guerlain Mitsouko, which, for some inexplicable reason, always reminds me of Damascus' palaces. I always open the tiny bottle very carefully, avoiding at all costs the excessive evaporation of that precious aroma, and then, eye closed, I take a deep breath to relive the vivid image of my mother. In that image, she is getting ready for my father, barefooted, semi-undressed, putting on her makeup in front of the bathroom mirror, one of those with large light bulbs around it that he brought from Paris. She seems so incredibly happy, as if that evening was their first date as an innocent couple, as if her feeling of love, unlike this perfume, was not ephemeral.

Another photograph that transports me to the past is the one I took of them, from behind, with my Polaroid camera as they walked toward the car after helping me move my things to my new student residence at Oxford. I was eighteen, and I had a whole trail of dreams in front of me; they were fifty-something and leaving behind a whole trail of dreams already lived, a trail leading all the way to their main dream: me. They were holding each other around the waist, and I remember thinking "that is love." I remember spending the entire afternoon locked in my room, crying inconsolably, terrified of having to now grow independently and by myself. Meanwhile, my mother was crying too, believing that I was celebrating my emancipation. Nowadays, there are still moments when I weep because I would give anything to go back in time and exchange that chimerical autonomy for remaining sheltered under the protective wings of that wise swan. Why do we rush to abandon our mothers?

The final photograph inside the box is of you: the love of my life. I never thought I would treasure a photo of us together with the memories of the past, because we always represented the present and, above all, the future. Yet there it is... framing us in a perfectly rectangular format, with the temples of Angkor in the background, you carrying me in your arms, looking satisfied, as if you were thinking, "Look at the big fish I caught," while I look similarly happy, happily trapped in your loving net. This black-and-white photograph reminds me that life is precisely that: light and shadows.

Before returning the photographs to the box, I find the wedding rings. Not ours, because we never got married after more than a decade together, but those of my parents. As though in an act of necromancy, I put a ring on the ring finger of each hand and then intertwine my fingers as though trying to resuscitate a caress between my parents. I tell myself again: yes, this is how love feels.

Finally, I place on the table the most difficult object of all for me to reconcile. It's a piece of paper on which my father—already hospitalized and facing his final hours—scribbled something indecipherable, something that filled me with doubt for the rest of my life. I always chose to believe this drawing was that of two overlapping hearts, my mother's and mine, until one day, she mysteriously said, with darkness in her eyes, "I wish those were our hearts." I never managed to decipher this enigmatic phrase or whether the expression in her glassy eyes was of love or a lack of it. Similarly, I will always be haunted by my father's decision to reject treatment, letting that damn malignant tumor devour everything. If he loved us so much, why did he not fight for his life? Why did he not fight for us? I imagine love is both mystery and revelation, tempest and calm, confession and silence (and sometimes confessions that should have remained silence).

I suppose love is confusing, especially when it feels right to love the wrong person and wrong to love the right one. I suppose love is poetry, sometimes made up of free verse that sounds chaotic, while at other times in perfect rhyme, although sounding less free. I suppose love is to say "I love you" even if you don't feel it, or to say nothing because you feel it too much. I suppose love is the medicine the soul needs, although sometimes it turns out to be intoxicating, with more love the only antidote, which might turn out to be lethal. I suppose the sentiment of love is a tremendous mystery to humanity itself that perhaps could be easily solved if we simply stopped calling it love and, instead, called it something else, such as *mirage*, *conquest*, or simply *magic spell*. I suppose love is so many things at the same time that it becomes convoluted and impossible to dissect, even when it comes from us, and even when we come from it.

# CHAPTER THREE

## PHNOM PENH

When I landed in Phnom Penh, Cambodia's capital, I had the usual feeling: they changed the country again! I'd always had a love-hate relationship with this country. Although I never felt any true connection with it, the reality is that I was addicted to it, and that's probably why I kept coming back after almost two decades. Phnom Penh was a city of contradictions, with its stinking streets and tasty durian fruit, its affable but cold-hearted people, its pagodas that looked fabulous from afar but were ultimately revealed to be made of poor-quality cement upon closer inspection. Cambodia was the country where we enjoyed our first adventure in the tropics, and there was no street, market, or plinth that didn't remind me of you. There wasn't a single corner that we hadn't turned or a streetlight along the riverside that hadn't illuminated our walks on the warm evenings. There was no barge in the Mekong on which our dreams had not floated, and there was no October rain that hadn't soaked us both.

When the *tuk-tuk* from the airport arrived at my hotel, I did something unexpected: I improvised. I catapulted the suitcases into the reception area and asked the driver not to leave just yet. When I returned, I asked him to take me directly to the wharf at the riverside. There it was... imperishable, iconic, timeless—the Kanika Boat, the most popular boat on the Mekong, frequented by lovers craving to perish of love under those legendary sunsets tinted in vanilla and guava shades that always reminded me of the ice-creams of my childhood. If only that boat could speak to tell all those tourists about our magical on-board confessions among the nocturnal fireflies...

I didn't hesitate to board the boat. On the river, hundreds of other smaller boats drifted sleepily, ferrying fishermen wearing silky *kramas* around their necks and conical reed hats that made them all resemble a bunch of mushrooms. The faint rattling of the engines from the other boats invited me to close my eyes and dream that this was the sound of an old film projector and that on the screen of my present life, the première of my fictitious past life was being staged against the backdrop of colonial French Cambodia. And, since dreaming was allowed, I frivolously dreamed that I was liberated and half naked, and that I was floating over those waters, lying on a huge barge built with wood and the love of four hands, and that I was drifting along the river toward Lake Tonle Sap, with the mystical Angkorian temples as the final destination. I dreamed myself infinite and ethereal, with no burdens, no mortgages, no goods; without expecting any dividend from life other than the pleasure of not having expectations. I dreamed myself awake and lucid, immune to the vibrations other vessels left in their wake. I dreamed myself taking a different course, neither better nor worse, just different. And I think that I even wanted to live life differently, not because I was unsatisfied with how it was, but because it is always difficult to come to terms with the idea of living just one life. So, I dreamed of waking up every morning as a new woman.

On the boat's deck, the couples cuddled in fervid demonstrations of love. Giving my imagination free rein, I began to imagine the messages and whispers couples in love share aboard these boats in the golden hour. A couple by the bow caught my attention. He was offering her a glass of white wine together with the promise of his infinite love; meanwhile, she was smiling at him, wondering whether life would always feel like a magical cruise. There by the bow, he kept on promising her clear skies and a wonderful future, undisturbed by any turbulence brought about by the propellers of life, or the typical whirlpools formed when the river narrows.

And while he kept on talking about the wonders of that future, by his side she was pulling, one by one, the petals of a lotus flower, which she threw into the river, perhaps to check whether they could float on their own words. Looking at each other through the kaleidoscope of life, they were turning around and around, surprising themselves by realizing how many shapes and colors that same love could take. She whispered forbidden things in his ear, while he stared at the starboard waters, pinching himself to believe his own unexpected good fortune for having found her, hoping that it would remain like this forever and that those erotic verses would continue to rhyme when the kaleidoscope stopped spinning. How wonderful the wonderful things couples say on those cruises.

Amused, she placed over his ear what was left of her leafless lotus flower; he remained stoic, without making any gesture of discomfort for that offense to his manhood.

There by the bow, she enjoyed herself, torturing the limits of his love for her. Then, testing love's limits, he approached her, whispering even more forbidden things in her ear, and she reacted tenderly, placing her hands over his eyes as if preventing him from glimpsing things that were not on offer. The games you play and become immersed in aboard those sunset cruises are mystical.

Meanwhile, at the other end of the boat another couple stood apart. They simply didn't talk.

From Silk Island, Phnom Penh resembled a deceptively calm anthill. Since the times when you and I first contemplated those same sunsets, tall skyscrapers had been built. The Royal Palace, always illuminated by festive lights, seemed cornered against the river, threatened by the inexorable advance of modernity —perhaps the very same modernity that pushed us as a couple into the abyss. That modernity of right angles instead of harmonious curves, of clinical syntax, the fierce enemy of phrases sown with adjectives and metaphors; that modernity made of concrete and cables, where the elegant lichens are no longer allowed to ornament the facades over time.

Like the couple by the bow, there was a time when you and I also felt invincible and filled with irreducible love. Perhaps that was our most fatal tactical error: to forget that love is like an ember that consumes itself with its own passion. But before the extinction of our love —just like the lovers by the bow— we used to promise each other a dream-filled future and hopeful winds; a future that, when it came, would only bring the longing for a past we wished to have enjoyed more while it was the present. There by the bow of our own ship, we also felt in command of a certain future, only later to discover that the future is the most uncertain and unguaranteed part of life. But, until we realized that, we also admired that romantic canvas of Phnom Penh at sunset. Those were the times when we too spread lotus petals over the river and where each petal that floated was a dream meant to come true. Not all those petals floated with the current, but it was nice not to be afraid to try. Now I am. And I believe I am because now I know that love is everlasting, while it lasts.

When the boat arrived back at the pier, and after having discreetly observed that lovely couple throughout the cruise, I couldn't avoid approaching them to say, "Do you see that quiet couple at the other end? Don't panic if one day you feel invaded by an overwhelming calm as well. It's fine. There are stretches of life when one is allowed to navigate in silence." Understandably, both looked perplexed. But there might be a day when they'll understand (and even agree).

After the boat trip, I dreaded being welcomed at the hotel by that ghost called solitude; so I decided to dodge my laptop and the many messages to be answered and sought refuge in the legendary Foreign Correspondents Club, the FCC. The lemon-color three-story colonial building with very wide windows —almost no walls at all— overlooks the river. It's the perfect place to transport yourself back into history and relive those epic moments from the past, where war was waged on the outside and not on the inside. The Vietnam War was chronicled by war correspondents and humanitarian personnel at the FCC. From its high ceilings, large fans hang, displaying noble wood blades that resemble the helicopters that once flew over the city. On the walls, large photographs show the fall of the city on April 17, 1975, to that guerrilla force dressed in black, the Khmer Rouge, who pointed rifles at their own people while shooting hatred through their eyes. It's hard to imagine the panic assailing those same streets only a handful of years before, amid the noise of motorcycles, music, and fun that now takes over every corner of the city. It's almost impossible to reconcile the fact that on that multicolored night not long ago, the longest night had darkened everything for several years. And yet it was true: the country once endured one of the most atrocious genocides that humanity has ever experienced.

I sat next to the window ledge overlooking the riverside and ordered my favorite Cambodian dish, fish *amok*, and a Tiger beer without ice. I devoted myself to examining the tourists while enjoying the fresh breeze. I started indulging in my favorite pastime: imagining the lives of others, something I used to do in my many moments of solitude. At one end of the bar there was a Cambodian girl with straight, silky hair and the abdomen of a mermaid. She had long eyelashes and the fragile fingers of a ballerina. Any innocent soul, unexposed to that environment, could have confused her with an *apsara*, or even with a disguised princess. And that's how she looked but for one almost imperceptible detail: she was drinking the cocktail of a whore (one of those sugary multicolored mocktails). At the other end of the bar was a fifty-year-old Australian tourist who feverishly gazed at that sublime sea creature, presumably thinking about how fortunate he was because she was watching him with reciprocal attention. He, of course, was drinking beer with ice, like every newcomer tourist.

Later, I noticed an elderly couple who looked at each other with unusual passion, almost fanatically, I would say.

They giggled, they tickled each other, they were even being playful like proper teenagers. They were constantly kissing, and not exchanging clinical pecks —the ones where you close your lips tightly to avoid salivating on the other— but instead sharing long and deep kisses, which even I judged as unhygienic. When they suddenly started to feed their fish *amok* to each other, with grains of rice falling down their chests, I felt an irrational and childish rage. If the magic of my relationship was over after fifteen years, why should theirs survive up to this point?!

I felt restless and began to wonder if my entire love life was not a tremendous failure. But... what if that elderly couple was not really in the winter of their relationship but rather in a new spring? I swiftly persuaded myself that she was probably a widow and he was divorced; that she brought along the sometimes-unexpected flame of new widows, while he brought the spark of finally having fulfilled the commitments that came with a forty-year marriage. That she had finally dropped the misconceived notion that sex was for reproduction and was now actively looking to rejoice in enjoying sex and having orgasms, while he had ultimately discovered that pleasing a woman in bed —and not the pension fund— was the best long-term investment. I felt deeply relieved with my own explanation of why this wasn't a miracle but a second chance, and, as my inner cosmos was being rebalanced, I heard a voice behind me: "Either that... or they are in their sunny winter."

I hesitated for an instant, unsure whether those words came from inside or outside my mind. After a few seconds, I couldn't resist the temptation and I spun around.

"Sometimes it happens," said the voice. "Not often, but sometimes it does happen."

"What happens?" I asked him without blinking.

After a pause for reflection, the mysterious man spoke: "Once upon a time, I transplanted some old olive trees. They looked pretty naked with almost no branches, nor leaves, nor roots. On top of that, I forgot to water them once I had planted them, and, the following year, they looked like fossilized trunks. Bare and dry trunks. I reckoned they were dead. But just as I was going to pull them out, someone asked me if I had checked if they were still green under the bark. When I scratched the bark with my fingernail, I discovered that several of them were still green. I watered them well, and the following year they grew twigs and some beautiful leaves. Sometimes it happens, not always, but sometimes it happens."

"And what did you do with those that were still dry?" I asked, accepting the surrealism of the situation.

"Those I pulled out."

I returned to my initial position without saying another word. I was confused both by the intrusion of that enigmatic man and by the fact that he seemed to be reading my mind. Then he went on speaking from behind me: "Sometimes it happens when the children finally leave home, or when one discovers with horror the first frosts of aging, or when the poacher is left with no more arrows for furtive activities. Whatever... Anything... Sometimes, the lightest puff can reignite the numb embers."

Without further delay, I got up and left.

The next morning, I decided to walk up to the World Bank offices along King Norodom's Avenue. The heat was suffocating even at that early hour. On the way, I enjoyed watching the colorful groups —mostly elderly people— who exercised their light bodies with gymnastics and monotonous choreography to the rhythm of strident music. I was tempted to join one of those groups, as I used to do in the past, and to feel like an apsara once again, but then I thought it was time to stop doing spontaneous and foolish things. I couldn't always be carried away by instinct. I wondered whether life should be lived backwards and that death should come with that first spanking just as we are born. And as that very thought came to mind, I turned around and decided to join the group anyway, entrusting my laptop to an old woman who I judged wouldn't run very far with it. The old woman shouted at me, "Good for the heart, and for incontinence!"

When I arrived at the World Bank, my clothes were soaked in sweat. I had my first meeting with Tim, the team leader, to follow up on the discussions held a few days earlier in Washington. We agreed that the project was complex, but we also considered the challenges worthwhile and that the chosen financing instrument, payment for results, had the potential to have a great impact in the desperate health context of Myanmar. The numbers spoke for themselves: over forty percent of children suffered from malnutrition, and almost one in ten children didn't reach the age of five.

Although the human drama was not so striking in the city, the rural areas had simply been left out of the so-called process of development. Even in the capital, massive social inequalities became apparent at first glance. Hundreds of children roamed the streets, looking for something to eat and chasing rats —sometimes for leisure, sometimes out of hunger— while luxurious sedans, including Rolls Royce models, parked next to piles of rubbish, with elegant men or women emerging from them, as if from another world.

Political tension in the country was running high after the highly contested elections, during which the previous government had been officially re-elected, but with a very narrow margin. However, the opposition party didn't recognize the results as legitimate and therefore had refused to take their seats in Parliament. The People's Party of Cambodia had ruled the country since shortly after the return to democracy, after the dark years of the Khmer Rouge, and its prime minister, Hun Sen, had emerged over the passage of time as a kind of supreme leader who ruled the country through an intricate and invisible spider web that reached every corner of every ministry, every business, and every transaction, lawful or not.

Bram, the regional director, had flown in from Bangkok the night before to attend a series of meetings at the highest level with the Ministry of Economy and Finance. The request for these meetings came from the government itself. It wasn't customary to involve the minister directly and to call our director without clarifying the specific reason for the meeting, although we had been unofficially told that the elephant in the room was not a request for financial support. Thus, a certain aura of mystery loomed over that meeting. Before leaving for the ministry, the team had a quick meeting at the Bank. This involved Bram; Daniel, the senior country economist; and me.

"How is your jet lag?" the director asked me.

"It's all right. I usually take melatonin pills," I answered.

"OK," Bram replied. "Today's agenda is— By the way, you already know each other, right?" he asked, referring to Daniel.

"Yes," we both replied.

Daniel and I had met a couple of times when he worked for the Inter-American Development Bank based in Washington, D.C.

"OK, so, what's the game plan?" Bram asked as he tied his tie.

That was, of course, a rhetorical question. Bram didn't like to improvise. He didn't do random. He was used to having the entire chess game mentally played several times before it had even begun. But on this occasion, he'd been invited to play by the government without knowing for certain what the game was all about or whether he was playing white or black. That kind of situation made him feel slightly nervous, because he was a square Austrian who regarded improvisation as a lack of sufficient planning.

The hierarchical order invited me to speak first. "What are the options?" I asked.

This question, also rhetorical, is what in the Bank's jargon is known as *the volleyball pass*. The principle is simple: never position yourself until you know what the commander in chief has in mind. Thus, Bram had signaled the commencement of the game, throwing the ball to the midfield. I received the ball, bouncing it into the air again, and the third in turn had no choice but to commit himself to some direction.

Daniel replied, "Maybe they finally decided to borrow from us?"

Daniel's ball went straight out.

"The government already agreed on a loan from China a few months ago worth almost a billion dollars. What would the need be to borrow more from us?" Bram asked, visibly disappointed with the lack of depth from the senior country economist.

"To learn how to spend it?" I replied.

Bram stared at me with the eyes of an old fox. He knew I never spoke without making sure of what I was saying.

"Feminine intuition?" he asked.

"No. Practice manager, and more years of experience in the Bank than anyone in this room."

The director didn't expect such a blunt response. He probably quickly realized that we were living in the whirlpool of an authentic gender revolution. Human Resources had spent millions on training and sensitization campaigns to tackle gender issues. Bram's remark, which might have gone unnoticed a decade earlier, could have now resulted in an accusation of sexual harassment.

"I imagine there's only one way to know," Bram said. "I mean what the government's request is, of course," he added, smiling, as he stood up, ready for the meeting.

Driving in the official vehicle, it was difficult to make our way through streets that had suddenly become a flood of protesting people. Thousands of youngsters were demonstrating against the government. Some were on foot, others on motorcycles; some carried flags with the colors of the opposition party, others Cambodian flags; some made noise blowing whistles, others tooted the horns of their motorcycles. Their banners carried slogans such as "Democracy for Cambodia," "Time for a change," and "Your moment has passed." When we reached Kampuchea Krom Avenue, I had the frightening sensation that we were in a war zone. Barricades with barbed wire blocked the demonstrators, and behind them, several rows of policemen and soldiers in riot gear lined up in perfect Roman formation to ensure that the youth, armed with whistles and longings for change, didn't reach Parliament.

Our vehicle suddenly became immersed in the human tide. The din was chilling, and had it not been for the inoffensive look of those faces still covered in acne and pure love, I would have felt terrified to be buffeted about like a scarecrow. Most of these young men and women had not even known the horrors of the Khmer Rouge; for them, that past was some sort of rumor that floated around the house like a ghost. Something unspoken but that must have existed; otherwise, Grandma wouldn't sit decorating the corner of the hut with her eyes lingering on the ceiling like a corpse, nor would Dad throw himself to the floor screaming every time someone approached him from behind, nor would Mom wake soaked in sweat every night. Those were the offspring of a traumatic past, who didn't know what to live under a government other than that was like, but who sensed that there could be a better one. Hundreds of faces crowded behind our car's windows, perhaps wondering who the hell we were and if we were with them or against them. I asked myself that very same question. When the police officers identified our license plates, they quickly let us through to the other side of the barricade.

Once at the Ministry of Economy and Finance, we were accommodated in the lobby of the minister's office and offered tea in porcelain cups. Another porcelain bowl displayed lychees in the center of a solid wooden table with a lacquer finish, which made it look like most modern Asian things: artificial. Only three pictures hung on the walls: a photograph of the new king, King Norodom Sihamoni; a photograph of his recently deceased father, the iconic Norodom Sihanouk, and his mother; and finally one of the prime minister, Hun Sen. The minister received us with courtesy, and, skipping the protocol, came up to the waiting room to accompany us to the meeting room, where other officials waited for us. It was a huge room, with high ceilings and a well-polished table that extended to infinity. His Excellency was considered by many a reformer, within a government full of mummies and other historical vestiges who, although having played a decisive role during the democratic transition, nowadays were mere relics in a Cambodia that demanded change. The secretary closed the windows, silencing the screaming of protesters on the street.

"Doctor Gipani," greeted the minister, "you are one of the few faces from the Bank that I keep seeing despite the passage of time. I still remember when you were a mere consultant, always rushing to take the minutes in the meetings. My country is indebted to you for your continued support, even though you now live on the other side of the world. I hope the Americans treat you well."

Bram felt uncomfortable not being the first one addressed by the minister. He proceeded to speak without being invited: "And we thank you for requesting our help, which we will gladly provide."

The minister smiled. "You westerners always put the ox before the cart... We cannot jump into business neglecting the courtesies, Mister Bram." He looked at his team, who smiled back in agreement.

Bram smiled bitterly.

"Daniel, *amigo mio*!" the Minister exclaimed in Spanish, surprising everyone. "When are we going to repeat that paella with Cambodian rice?"

Intrigued, Bram and I looked at Daniel, who swiftly regained the confidence lost during the pre-meeting. I couldn't help thinking about you and your unorthodox Latin manners that always worked so well for you.

"Well," said the minister, "it's no secret that these are politically challenging times. The opposition falsely claims that the results from the last elections were altered and refuse to take their seats in Parliament. We have not had a normal parliamentary life for months now. But that leader of the opposition," he said, his face stiffening, "seems not to care about his own country, perhaps because he spends half of his self-exiled life in Paris."

"What is the government's strategy to shift the status quo?" Bram asked.

The minister stood up from his comfortable chair and slowly walked along the table to reach the other side, where we sat. He offered us tea and ceremoniously filled our cups himself, one by one. Then he returned to his seat and sank into silence for a few seconds.

"Do you practice any martial arts, Mr. Bram?" the minister asked.

Bram shook his head. It was well known that His Excellency was a karate expert with several trophies in his showcase. The minister continued: "In politics, as in martial arts, patience is everything. One must wait for one's opportunity, Mr. Bram, without rushing. One waits,

waits, waits... and, when the time comes: one punch, one kill!"

The atmosphere became tense with the comment, which he staged with his own belligerent hands. Remembering the Cambodia of the eighties, where the purging of opponents was a frequent activity, inevitably came to mind.

"But, of course, we have not asked you to come to talk about fighting, but about how the World Bank can help us improve, or rather, how you can help the country to prosper," the minister said, now more affable.

Bram's face lit up when he realized that the Cambodian government might be willing to take up the loan offered by the Bank a year before. "You well know, minister, that the government is our only client, and that our offer is still on the table.

The minister smiled. "It's not that kind of help we need right now, Mr. Bram. For support of that nature, we already have other friends who, incidentally, offer their friendship with rather less conditionality, to put it mildly," the minister said, smiling at his colleagues.

The geopolitical game was complex in those years. China was granting large amounts of credit to countries in the region, and it was difficult to compete against promptly disbursed money, with few or no ties attached, at least initially. The loans and concessions made by the World Bank had very low interest rates and comfortable repayment facilities, but the money trail was heavily audited to minimize corruption and the funds were often disbursed against results. The times of blank checks were over.

"What we need from the World Bank is to help us to reform this country," added the minister. "We want to reform each and every one of the sectors, starting with those that have the greatest impact on poor people: health, education, and social protection. And we also want to generate more industry, be like our Thai and Malaysian neighbors, not only make T-shirts but also assemble hard drives and mobiles. There is no other institution with the technical and analytical capacity that you have."

The request seemed genuine. The reasons why they wanted to reform the country from top to bottom just at that moment was another matter. I looked sideways at Bram and saw how he was initially dismayed to hear that the government didn't have the intention to borrow from us. It was understandable: a regional director was appraised by our own institution mainly based on the volume of loans granted. However, he soon adopted a more positive look when he perceived the magnitude of the operation. I decided to speak up: "Is the government also willing to reform the procurement of pharmaceuticals?"

My question took the minister and his colleagues by surprise —and Bram and Daniel, who looked at me, shocked by my direct approach and my mention of the matter without having previously consulted the team on the strategy we would follow. The Ministry of Health had refused before to discuss the issue openly, although behind doors they confessed to us that the issue was at a very high level, even beyond their own jurisdiction.

The minister looked at the colleague on his right and then on his left, and somewhat embarrassed said, "I'm afraid that's quite a minefield..."

Daniel, encouraged by the impression that the government was really willing to engage, asked, "Is the government also considering reforms in the trade sector, such as streamlining customs processes and eliminating middleman costs?"

The minister nodded again, making it clear that they were willing to reform (almost) everything. They were really desperate, I thought. I had never seen them that vulnerable before. The very tight victory in the last general elections had put them on the edge of the abyss after decades of government secured by divine mandate.

"Our request to the World Bank," said the minister, "is that you come back to us within two weeks with a proposal listing three reforms for each sector. We will then decide how to proceed."

Both Bram and Daniel were excited by the scale of the proposal and the theoretically positive impact this could have on a country with tremendous potential, whose burden had precisely been the lack of sufficient reforms in the last years. Our director was about to intervene, but I took the lead, posing a question I knew violated the Bank's number one rule of putting pressure on a government only if it wouldn't make them lose face: "Why now? Why in two weeks?"

Bram glanced at me, visibly angry, while the minister stared at me with respect, even with admiration, I would say, for my courage. The World Bank simply does not allow internal dissidence. After a sincere silence that was almost confessional, His Excellency concluded the meeting with, "In two weeks, please."

As we left the room, the minister shook our hands, one by one, and, when my turn came, he skipped the protocol, pulled me aside, and, with a rather paternalistic tone, said, "Evolution, Doctor, not revolution."

Once the three of us were away from the eyes of the ministry officers, Bram exploded. Hitting the table with his briefcase, he shouted, "What the hell was that about? Gipani, you simply cannot come all the way from Washington to question this government's motives so disrespectfully!"

"And you shouldn't come all the way from Bangkok to award yourself a medal without questioning anything. We are not mercenaries!"

Bram removed his glasses and massaged his temples, while Daniel watched us, applying to himself another of the Bank's golden rules: do not get involved unless necessary.

"I don't get you, Gipani, I really don't. You have been with this institution for almost two decades. You know the rules of the game. I made it very clear in the videoconference: we don't get involved in political considerations; we simply work with the government that has been democratically elected.

"Tell *them* that!" I shouted as I violently pushed the windows wide open.

The protests in the streets had become more agitated, and police officers were by then running after demonstrators, dispersing them with tear gas and rubber balls.

"You know exactly what we are being asked to do here, right?" I said to a director not used to being contradicted in that way. "What they expect from us is to clean up their image so that they can win the next general elections and then go back to business as usual."

"And what are we supposed to do? Let the country sink back into the Middle Ages?" Bram said.

"I don't know but hindering natural evolution certainly won't help. That's not development."

Daniel tried to reconcile the opposing positions: "I'm afraid development is a double-edged sword."

Bram buried his face in his hands, and said in despair, "Now we're becoming all philosophical. What a pity that a director cannot afford to do that."

That night I went back to the Foreign Correspondents Club for dinner. I had to refuse several invitations because I couldn't bear the pain of having to talk about work in my leisure time. I went alone, and I sat by the veranda, in my usual corner overlooking the riverside. A pearl-colored full moon tinted the roofs of every pagoda in town, while endless neon lights sputtered down the street along the promenade by the river. The barges came and went through the Mekong, releasing dead sounds and mystical vapors that would remain floating on the water. Small groups of youngsters in cars passed from time to time, leaving snatches of political chants and festive whistles in their wake. I assumed they came from the demonstration and were delaying going home, where only the daily misery awaited them.

"Evolution, not revolution." The minister's words echoed in my mind. Maybe he was right, although at that moment I would have gladly joined that mob, captaining the revolt for freedom. I don't know… Perhaps, it was all because my heart was also longing for change and craved fresh air. I felt rebellious and, for some strange reason, erotic at the same time.

At the end of the bar —timelessly— was the same whore drinking the same cocktail of whores. This time, however, I didn't want to make presumptions about her life; this time, I wanted to see what her reality looked like. In the blink of an eye, she was sitting next to me, fluttering her false eyelashes. She wore a dress covered in turquoise-green sequins. She had the long legs of a young filly and a nacre skin that matched her long porcelain nails. I didn't ask her for her name or occupation. What for? Both answers would have been false. Instead, I asked her if she had ever been in love. The question caught her by surprise, and in her clumsy attempt to disguise her restlessness, she took my glass of white wine and drank it in long sips. When she realized her mistake, she was attacked by nervous, uncontrolled laugher. The woman became a girl. I ordered a bottle of the same wine and two glasses.

"How can one know that?" she asked me.

Now it was her who took me by surprise. Deliberately, I drank my wine in long sips, mimicking her previous gesture. The girl spontaneously rested her face on my shoulder. She laughed again, her body contorting which made her ribs quite prominent. After so many years in Washington, I was no longer used to casual physical contact, and my instinct was to remain still like a statue. I looked around and spotted two men staring at us. Strangely, I felt powerful knowing that I could control their libido from a distance.

I tried to explain, in the simplest possible manner, what I believed being in love felt like: "I think you know if you're in love because of the flitting butterflies in your stomach."

"Butterflies?" The girl said, reflecting on my description, before ducking her head. "No, no butterflies for me..."

I felt compassion for her. I thought it was cruel, not only because she did not know what true love felt like but also because she almost certainly never would. Although, in all fairness, it also seemed heartless to feel loved and then lose it, and even more painful to live under the impression that what you feel is love, and ultimately discover that it is not, that it is something else.

The girl added, "Well... yes, I know what love is: my mother's love."

I found the comment tender, and even more so because of the way she said it. I clinked my glass against hers. But shortly after, she added that her mother also loved her two other little sisters, but, since she was the oldest one and there was no breadwinner at home, at the age of sixteen her mother had to sell her to an Australian *barang* (foreigner), who soon abandoned her —while she was carrying a baby in her womb.

I didn't need to hear the rest of her story to anticipate that life would have forced her to go through all sorts of temporary badly paid jobs, only to finally discover that the easiest way to open her own company was to open up herself. But, that evening, neither of us had the appetite to descend into the underground of our own lives, where the ghosts and other demons hide. Instead, I suggested that she enjoy the evening, doing whatever she wanted to. "Let's get pretty," she swiftly replied.

She chose to go to one of those beauty salons that close at dawn to embellish the loving kittens of the night. We got all dressed up, wearing more makeup than necessary, just like the teenagers we felt like. Between laughter and revelry, the hairdressers made us up with whimsical painting and carnival glitter, fixed us with false eyelashes so long that they cast Chinese shadows, and adorned us with fantasy hair extensions. They took selfies with us, joining our festivities, while beautifying each other, contaminated by our excitement.

We ruled out going to all the bars and clubs that would remind her of what she did for a living, and, instead, we jumped from rooftop to rooftop, listening to happy music, dancing like crazy girls and drinking enthusiastically — unknown white wines for her; sugary cocktails for me, which at that point in time tasted like a great wine. The night kept spinning like a Ferris wheel that had come off its axis. An unrestrained desire to explore new horizons began to emerge, centrifuged in all directions. Several men wanted to invite themselves to our party. We let them believe in magic, for a while, until we eliminated them.

We decided to take refuge in Neverland, the amusement park. My new friend had confessed that her best childhood memory was when her mother took her and her sisters to the funfair, right there at the intersection between Sihanouk Boulevard and Sothearos Street. Her mother would spoil them, letting them each choose an attraction, and then she would buy one of those giant cotton candies for the three girls. She remembered the cotton candy as a magic cloud on which her happiness turned rosy.

I did the same and asked the boy to weave the largest cotton candy he possibly could. It became so unbelievably gigantic that it generated an infinite queue of parents demanding the same treatment for their puppies. Trying to make up for her interrupted childhood, I invited her to ride each and every one of the park's attractions. We rode in the crazy jumpy frog, in the impetuous bouncing grasshopper, and in the surreally jittery octopus.

Because of all those crazy jumps, my friend gradually lost her feline eyelashes, her night-lady heels, her large hoop earrings. As she did so, she regained her authentic skin, the freshness of the hidden girl, the spirit that had strayed along the labyrinth of her own life. By the time she had become herself, and I was almost myself, I had already subconsciously taken the role of her boyfriend. So, I tried my luck with the darts, and I tried throwing balls against tin cans. The only reason I didn't shoot with the cowboy rifle was because I had recently collected signatures to regulate the use of arms in the United States.

We left our playground feeling different, having changed. We walked out as lovers do when exiting the funfair: she with a huge teddy bear, me eating nuts. It must have been as late as four in the morning. A fresh, bluish full moon, crowned with a halo, hung at the zenith of the sky. The night was young, and the streets were still full of joy and good desires.

We walked barefoot along the riverside, carrying our high heels in hand —always a symbol of a long and successful night. We ended up sitting on a bench where the boats dock. And there it was: that majestic river cruise, the one that you and I regretfully never dared jump on, still floating over a mystical fog from the past. I'm not completely sure what happened to me then. Maybe it was meeting up again with that dream cruise that you and I so often fantasized boarding to set sail towards the mystery of ourselves (as you used to say); or, perhaps, it was the excess of wine and new sensations, I don't know... but suddenly I found myself immersed in an ocean of tears, which condensed in a flurry of abrupt confessions to a perfect stranger. I confessed how much I needed you, how much I had loved you, and, foremost, how much I could love you again.

I told her all this, while she strangely commenced to sing in my ear with her honeyed, mermaid voice. I told her about your perennial caresses and your breezy touch over my naked skin while she blew on my hands with her warm breath. I told her about our ethereal dreams while she closed my eyelids with her confident fingertips. And, just when I began to fear that I was moving through quicksand, and my senses were alerting me of the risk of confounding love for desire, she whispered in my ear, "You know what you should do? Get on that boat and go straight, straight, until you find the butterflies."

# CHAPTER FOUR

## THE RIVER FLOWS IN YOU

I did it. I finally did it. I boarded that ship that so many times we let sail without us. Phnom Penh to Siem Reap, four days and three nights cruising the mystical Mekong River. There it was: docked at the riverside, chained to time, condemned to sail without us. That's how I found the old colonial ship at sunrise: with its golden insignia of the *Compagnie Fluviale du Mékong*, with its aura from other times, with its inspiring name: *Nouveau Printemps* (New Spring). It was a relic from old glories, its cabins decorated with noble woods, capable of transporting anyone back to that glorious and delicate past. It was a trip destined for a mirage —undoubtedly— that I wouldn't have minded myself or you reflected in, if there is at all any difference. The truth is that it doesn't matter, because that morning, I finally set sail on our boat, even when you were not on it, even when I might not be myself on it either.

I still remember how much we loved those charming sunsets over the waters of the Mekong, where the four arms of the river converge —Tonle Sap and Tonle Bassac— a gorgeous postcard with a reddish and diaphanous sun setting behind the walls of the Royal Palace, creating flares around everything with its passionate touch. Similarly revealing were the sunsets after an October storm. Then, the atmosphere turned polychromatic, the scent of the wet earth became more prominent than ever, and one discovered that it is in life, and not in death, where one can best enjoy the kingdom of heaven.

I still retain in my pupils the stamp of all those firmaments in general, but one in particular with almost artificial vanilla shades. Under that surreal sky, you told me, "Don't be surprised if one day, and hopefully that day never comes, you find in the reasons to love me the very same reasons to hate me." Back then, I interpreted your mysterious sentence as one more of those phrases said when one is deeply in love, totally disregarding any overt messages. Yet when the time came (and it did come), I unfortunately understood its full meaning.

Anyway… I also vividly remember how, just before boarding one of those small boats, you normally used to pause, hypnotized, looking at that other glamorous boat, which I had boarded that morning, and you dreamed, I think, that your life was that of someone else. That of a bohemian or a writer perhaps —anything but a World Bank official working in trade. One day you proposed that we get on that ship and never set foot on land again, let alone in reality. And repeating a passage from my favorite novel, I replied, "And how long do you think we can keep up this goddamn coming and going?" You also had an answer ready for years, but instead of telling me what you had in mind, you winked at me, and we simply drifted with the current.

Now, instead of letting life drag me along, it was me who dragged life to that place: the river docks. At seven in the morning, a *tuk-tuk* picked me up from the hotel and unloaded me, together with my suitcase, at the riverside. I felt good. I felt very good, indeed. Perhaps it was the feeling of freedom. A service boy escorted me up to my cabin on the upper deck, carrying my wheeled suitcase, instead of dragging it, to avoid scratching the glossy floor. Once in the room, he slid open the heavy wooden door for me to enjoy the private balcony overlooking the river.

The early morning sunbeams enticed me to the party of life, and, in full celebration, I imprudently leaned over the railing of the balcony to bathe myself in its flaring light. The boy, presumably thinking that I intended to jump into the river, shouted, "Be careful, ma'am, there are fish with giant mustaches in the Mekong!" meaning that there were giant fish with whiskers. I smiled, although, in all fairness, it wasn't his fault but rather mine for my still limited command of the Khmer language, after so many years visiting that country. A dollar tip made him smile as well, and, after he shut the door, I collapsed on my queen-size bed for one.

I snuggled up like a little girl —I think I also wanted to be one— letting the sunlight heat my bare feet. I always found pleasure in having my feet rest on the edge of the mattress, to let my sandals slide off, one after the other, until I felt stripped of everything. For some strange reason, I always found this to be a liberating gesture, even suggestive. The wooden frame of the balcony perfectly framed the scene of what Hun Sen's Cambodia had become: a black and white image. A high-contrast photograph with the luxurious hotel-casino Sokha in the background and the floating houses of the poor fishermen in the foreground. However, at that moment I didn't want to think about development, so, leaving politics aside, I rolled between the sheets, which emanated a strong scent of jasmine softener, until I finally fell asleep for more than an hour.

Due to the damn jet lag, I hadn't had much sleep the night before, and because of that, I missed the departure's preludes: the hoarse moaning of the horn, the release of the moorings, and the lifting of the heavy anchor, the captain's shouting of orders and the sailors' replies, the effusive exchange of farewells from the passengers on deck, the cheerful sound of the newly greased machines... The staging of life, in short. By the time I woke up, the Royal Palace visible in the distance seemed almost like a toy with which I could play a game of princes and princesses. I hesitated for a moment, caught between opening my laptop to check my e-mail and going on deck. I had not read my e-mail for almost two hours! Unprecedented... This frivolity made me feel guilty. I made a move to open my computer, but, suddenly, I felt panicked at being alone, and, in an act of visceral contempt, I threw the laptop against the pillow and rushed out of my cabin.

A bright light reflected on the freshly varnished wooden floor. Groping, light blind, I went up to the other side of the deck to open my eyes. Everything looked bluish, with a placid yet spiritual azure tinge. The musical notes from a *roneat* collided in the air with those from a *tron* in a welcoming song spreading from the bow of the boat. Guided by curiosity, I followed the trail of the melody, until I reached a large glass saloon, from which the melody spilled over the deck. The French-style decorations from the golden colonial times transported me to the days when

Phnom Penh was the pearl of Asia, and Asia a jewel in itself.

Three ballerinas, *apsaras* with porcelain faces, were staging the false romanticism of the rice field chores. Their hands flapped in the air while their fragile fingers defied their natural curves. Everything was hands. Hands intertwined, hands floating, dancing hands illuminated by the flashes of the tourist cameras. I became disillusioned with the prevailing demography: a crowd of grannies dancing, uncoordinated, to the sound of young rhythms. But what could I expect aboard a luxury vessel at the rate of six hundred dollars a night! I was about to leave, and I would have done so had it not been for another service boy suddenly putting a cup of lotus flower tea in my hands and saying, "I know what you're thinking, but wait, because you haven't seen it all yet."

Trying to overcome the initial disappointment, and in a desperate attempt to look at those tourists from a different perspective, I again played the game of imagining the tourists' past and present. A stout rosy-faced woman, sitting in the front row in a wicker chair beside her standing husband, took her husband's hand, placing it tenderly against her cheek while looking at him with jubilant eyes, presumably grateful for the surprise gift coinciding with their golden anniversary. A gay couple of autumnal age but spring feelings followed the group of spontaneous dancers. The more effeminate of the two reminded me of an old work colleague, also gay, who had the extrasensory perception of guessing with disconcerting reliability whether I had had sex the night before. That superpower became an added reason for me to request a transfer to another unit.

At the back of the room, a woman and a man exchanged glances intermittently. She smoked using a long cigarette holder, as though in the Paris of the thirties. I imagined she would be French, although later on I discovered that she simply wanted to be. He, meanwhile, kept on watching her sideways, then shied away whenever she turned to him. They continued playing this childish game until her long cigarette was finished, and his patience was too. Then, the two came out of the salon, instinctively following —almost chasing— each other, straight to her cabin, marked by urgency. I couldn't guess whether it was indeed an upset couple eager to be reunited or the product of an adventurous union after two divorces. In any case, I realized that I had perhaps rushed to judge the ecosystem onboard. The ship was, as its name suggested, flooded with love.

I finally escaped that musical glass box, and on the deck, I leaned back over the handrail. From my new position, I continued scanning the colorful crew who tried, with more passion than accomplishment, to imitate the graceful movements of the *apsaras*. I sipped tea from my cup and anxiously sought someone of my age with whom I could engage in conversation. No success. I took a look at my schedule, with the hopes to finding some teleconference planned for that morning. No luck there either. I even considered joining one of those videoconferences on nutrition and poverty offered on the intranet at lunchtime.

Just when I was about to suffer an acute attack of solitude, I spotted a mysterious character who had until then gone unnoticed among the crowd. He was also on deck, but on the opposite side, leaving the glass room as the only barrier between us. However, in the backlight, it was impossible for me to see his face and predict his age. The burst of light behind his back generated a mystical halo around him. In contrast, I was on the visible side, which left me at a tremendously irritating disadvantage. I couldn't see him well, but he could see me, and in great detail.

"I should have stayed in the cabin checking my e-mails," I criticized myself. From my position, I could only verify that he wore loose clothes of white cotton, which waved in the wind without conveying any information other than a sense of freedom. He seemed relatively tall and had light, copper-colored, curly hair. Later, I would discover that he had piercing hazel eyes, like two puddles of honey, and a mesmerizing gaze, which, alongside his voice, had sorcerous properties.

I thought of taking my phone out and walking, indifferently, toward him while pretending to be engaged in some sophisticated conversation, only to ignore him when passing, except for a quick, disarming glance. But I realized that there was no network coverage in that remote part of the river. I would come across as a complete idiot if he noticed; if he didn't, I would judge him as insufficiently intelligent. I thought of turning my back on him, to take out my dressing mirror and reflect some flashes to his face as if by accident, but my feminist side advised me not to use women's accessories for spurious purposes. It even occurred to me to go back into that room and dance like one more *apsara*, just as I had learned in a dancing course back in the day. The truth is that I could have done it, and it could have worked, but I simply didn't have the courage. Ultimately, half-consciously, foolishly, I raised my glass to him in a toast. I don't know how I dared to do such a thing. I cursed myself again and again for having done it. "But what do I do? He's going to think I'm desperate," I scolded myself. Fortunately, I believe my gesture went unnoticed, or, if he did notice it, he didn't react, which in a way was much worse, as I was not used to being ignored.

Disappointed with myself, and so that the stranger couldn't read my frustration, I turned back to face the river and rested my forearms on the railing. I closed my eyes and tried to empty my mind, trying to concentrate solely on my present perceptions. I first noticed the sound of my own breathing: breathing in, breathing out... After only a minute of listening to the monotonous sound of the air coming into and out of my lungs, I already felt purified of my foolish outburst. One minute, just one minute, listening to my own echo —to my own self— and I was already finding myself again. Then, the hollow rattling of flimsy fishing boats came, and, within a few seconds, the crashing of the waves raised against the hull of the ship. Two minutes later, carried by the wind, I smelt the sweet scent of gasoline and oil burning as it came out of the sad four-stroke engine and, with it, even sweeter memories of my childhood playing by the swamp. Three minutes later, the breeze detoxified the air again, and the fluvial humidity appeared again in my sense of smell, bringing with it the image of a fish with huge whiskers, which made me giggle. Four minutes later, a warm draft tickled my skin, giving me goosebumps, while the sun heated my forehead, yielding a pleasurable drowsiness that weakened my knees. Five minutes later, I was me again. That's all it takes: five minutes. And, yet, we don't grant ourselves even that small fraction of time in modern times.

Rivers have a hypnotic magic. I bumped into the memories of all those afternoons I used to sit in Port Meadow, on the fresh grass, to contemplate how the Isis River flows along its way. Rivers always seem the same, and yet they never are the same. In constant flow, they are continually changing. Just like we do. We tend to think of ourselves as stable personas, but we are also perpetually evolving. It seems almost a miracle to me when two persons who committed themselves in the past to stay together (based on who they were) later on recognize each other as who they were. How could anyone possibly decide in the past to remain together in the present?

Rivers make me drift. They also have the power to bring me floating past sensations. One of those sensations is that of time. Not the time of the watch's hands — measured in seconds— but of that invisible clock everyone carries inside that moves with its own notion. In time, just as in rivers, one can easily drown, or, worse, drift toward an unintended destination, from where swimming upriver becomes impossible. To find myself floating in the middle of a vast ocean, simply because I was cast adrift, because I was distracted by the daily chores or by someone else's visions, was always my deepest fear.

Sometimes I think of life as a beautiful time ladder with thousands of small rungs. I know, and I understand, that all of those small rungs are important and that without them that beautiful time ladder becomes dismembered and stop being beautiful. I endlessly remind myself that I must enjoy each and every one of those little rungs, which represent short but magical moments in life. I tell myself that the goal in life is not to reach that last rung in the ladder but to enjoy each and every one of those little steps:

life itself. I keep reminding myself that the ascent itself, and not reaching the summit, is the ultimate meaning of life. And, yet, I do not feel it that way. Damn it, I simply don't! And what a pity, and what a suffocating suffering not to feel that way... Maybe there was a time when I did, but not anymore. Now I think that in life there are only two or three rungs that really are crucial, and that all the other steps are only intermediaries, mere irrelevant transitions, just a linkage to those more decisive rungs; trivial steps, which are advisable to go over as fast as one possibly can. I know it's sad to think that way! And yet I can't help it.

I took a pen and I started writing down some random thoughts. I wrote: "Time is my greatest enemy." Time is the enemy of us all. We all try to resist the passage of time, that inevitable walk toward death. But my own struggle against time is of a different nature. My fight is against myself, against my own appreciation of time. Several years ago, while doing a psychometric test in Washington, D.C., for work, I discovered that my perception of one minute was exactly forty-three seconds. What was incredible was to prove that, after repeated measurements, my perception of time remained twenty-nine percent shorter than the average; in other words, I feel that life moves twenty-nine percent faster than most people do. Coming back to my reflection about the time ladder, it comes as no surprise then that I want to pass over those minor steps as quickly as possible, because deep down, I feel that life is not long enough to recreate myself in the little things.

What a condemnation to have to feel like that! I wish I could restart my own biological clock and calibrate it with that of the majority. However, in doing so, would I have achieved everything I have achieved? Maybe not. Perhaps, then, my distorted perception of time is not disadvantageous… Perhaps, I have accomplished various milestones twenty-nine percent earlier than most people of my generation. For example, I lost my virginity two years earlier than the average. I completed my doctorate three years before most. I built my first house before my peers had a mortgage. I was promoted to head of section at a record age. I even started living as part of a couple, and consequently was separated, before anyone else.

But since when has my perception of time been distorted? The truth is that I don't remember suffering from this condition when I was younger. For example, at the age of eleven, I used to spend endless evenings with my grandfather merely contemplating the sea. Sitting by the pier in Brighton, we would observe how the tide withdrew little by little, discovering giant blue rocks that resembled fantastic wrecks, on which crabs tinted in indigo colors would seek refuge until some naughty seagull swooped down on them, threading them with the beak. We would spend —literally— hours of sixty minutes (which by no means felt like forty-three minutes) counting how many of those crabs perished under the voracity of the seabirds, and how many gulls perished under the voracity of the boys who meanwhile entertained themselves with their slings. "One… two… three…!" That's how we counted them, aloud, until the sun set beyond that neutral line that separates the sea from the sky. And once we were done with the crabs, we would lie down, turning our attention to the sky to count the flickering stars, which revealed themselves one by one, timidly, as if asking for permission to exist.

And the best part was that I was there, and not only in body but in spirit too, with all five senses placed in the moment. I don't remember wanting to be somewhere else, much less thinking that I was wasting my time. Time was not important. It is now. Damn you, time! Similarly, later on as an adolescent, dozens and dozens of poetry books would pile up like Towers of Pisa in every corner of my parents' house. And once at college, more of the same: my appetite for the humanities never diminished, even if mixed with math or quantum physics. Why not? "One can't devour the universe without nourishing the soul first," I recall one of my professors from Wolfson College saying.

Back in those days, it was almost unthinkable to define oneself as an academic (or simply a person) without being able to sustain at least a light conversation on philosophy in a pub. I would even say that one had to be seen reading poetry in a pub to deserve having an ale! I recall how shocked the Harvard exchange students were to see how our illustrious Oxford scientists "wasted time" (in the exchange students' view) by talking about things other than numbers. Poor Harvard students! The roller of modernity had already passed over them... But things are changing everywhere, even in Oxford. Now, time has become a precious asset not to be wasted on impractical things. Readings that don't provide an average of ten tangible pieces of data per page are considered frivolous.

Modernity also ended up biting me. Those old Towers of Pisa have gradually been replaced by bundles of magazines like *The Economist* and *Time*. Magazines that, to tell the truth, I barely enjoy reading, but that represent indispensable instruments to start a coffee conversation at headquarters in D.C. What kind of conversation would you strike up with your colleagues otherwise? Flaubert? Zola? The mere gesture of carrying one of those forbidden books in my luggage feels inappropriate, and I would never dare exposing myself in public by lightheartedly reading a novel. We all seem to have succumbed to that black magic. On my last mission to Pakistan, after a long week of work, I surprised myself by feeling disgruntled when one Sunday I caught one of the consultants enjoying poetry by the hotel swimming pool, and with no apparent sign of remorse!

Later that afternoon, I went back on deck. The sunset was not one of those polychromatic wonders we used to admire together; instead, the sky was covered by a layer of thin clouds dully diffusing the light. Consequently, the waters of the Mekong didn't sparkle like the usual amalgam of silver and mercury at that time of the day. But I enjoyed looking at the half-naked children jumping from their houseboats into the river. Childhood by the river always tastes like childhood. Yet I often wonder if those smiley children are really happy. Sometimes, I tell myself that they aren't, that they may seem like it, or even (transiently) be, but, ultimately, their basic needs aren't covered and therefore they can't be as happy as most Western children. At those times I choose to believe that my work in development is fully justified. But then I think of many of those very same Western children —glued to televisions and dependent on their tablets— and my beliefs start to crumble. Anyhow, that day I didn't want to question my faith in development; instead, I simply delighted in contemplating the splash of those children in the river. I was a girl once; I was also happy in the river.

For the evening dinner on deck, I decided to put on the dress you used to say turns me into an Indian deity, the same one I wore when I fell in love with you on that twenty-fourth day of February between the temples of Angkor, the same one I wore when we promised ourselves —silently— an unconditional and eternal love. Sitting in the restaurant, waiting for supper, the fluvial breeze overwhelmed my senses. I was accommodated on a little old teak table next to the railing, from which I watched the fluorescent foam born from the propellers. I was alone. And available. And harboring an intense desire to stop being so. Why should a woman apologize for feeling this way? The sensation of freedom started crossing that always tenuous line that separates it from libertinism. The exotic background did nothing but to enhance this emotion.

The Khmer folklore had given way to a sax that transported me to French-colonial Cambodia, where the nights were long and vaporous. How much I craved having you with me then! But you were not, you simply were not... whereas that mysterious man was. He was sitting there in his corner, at a table similar to mine, with a candle that threatened to be extinguished by the breeze and a bottle of wine that didn't deserve to be drunk in solitude. I don't know why, but, again, that unjustified feeling that I've been dragging along since we broke up — that of infidelity— haunted me again. What we built was over, but yet you continue to accompany me like a ghost (for better or for worse). That evening, once again, you were next to me like a spirit, but that mysterious man was there in body and soul.

He drank from a wide glass while reading who knows what —surely not a financial report, because no one can smile as he did while reading that type of literature. He ate painfully slowly, as if time was his. Now I could affirm in all certainty that he had curly hair and that it was somehow longer than typically worn by a man in his mid-forties. Regarding his nationality, I presumed he might be either French or Italian, certainly anything but British. His passionate gestures, all hands in the air, didn't seem to me of an English cut, and neither were his linen Mediterranean clothes or rimless glasses. Intriguing…

I ordered a glass of white wine (Giro Ros, an author's wine), and I continued to observe how he delighted himself. He kept on reading and giggling, with occasional outbursts of contained laughter, to the point when I started feeling more curiosity about the content of his reading than about him. Suddenly, an extremely attractive waitress with a long heron-like neck approached him. There was an exchange of words between the two, with some unusually expansive gestures. He laid his broad hand over her delicate forearm, and she lost some of her Asian composure. And so they continued, for a couple of minutes, wrapped in a conversation of unquestionable flirtation. Had that occurred at the World Bank's headquarters, it would definitely be classified as sexual harassment. I must admit that I felt jealous.

When the waitress left, taking the dishes with her, the man quickly scanned around, catching me off guard while I stared at him owlishly. He smiled and raised his glass, toasted me from the other side. Out of pure feline instinct, I associated his unexpected toast with the one I had unconsciously exchanged with him on that very morning by the deck. "Is he making fun of me?" I wondered. The potential power imbalance made me feel uncomfortable.

I'd done so many of those courses on negotiation skills, and all for what? There were only one or two ways to reverse that hypothetical imbalance of power. I tried to identify an alternative, a man with whom to strike up a conversation. But there was none. A second strategy would have been to move to a more favorable terrain, which, on that boat, could have translated into moving to the veranda, and, contemplating the moon and the stars, portraying myself as ethereal and seductive to attract his attention. But what if he wouldn't make a move and I remained there under the stars looking dumb? I discarded this option. A third strategy consisted of simply leaving, and so I did. I sat on a deck chair and let myself be seduced by a waning moon that illuminated everything. After a few minutes, I heard his voice behind me: "Time and love; love and time —mutual enemies."

It was irritating. Not his style itself, but the fact that I was attracted to it. I promptly associated it with your own magnetism, your very same aura, you. However, I decided to ignore him. I remained impassive, as if I had not heard a word. After a few minutes, without turning back, I finally asked, "Are you still there?"

The voice took a few moments to respond. "No." A few seconds later he added, "Well, physically yes, but my confidence no longer."

That simple casual gesture made me lower my defenses, but entrenched in my strategy, I said nothing. His English was perfect, although with unequivocal French traces that, again, reminded me of your romance accent and how that made you seem more exotic. I couldn't help it: I simply melted. His hard breathing at my back, his powerful scent spreading everywhere, his mere masculine presence... I cursed myself for finding it so irresistible.

"Are you afraid of time?" I asked.

"Not as much as I fear love," he replied.

I waited for him to elaborate. He did. "Love expires with time, and time becomes eternal without love."

His words fell like a scourge on my soul. He was right. I didn't want to admit it, but he was right. During our cold sentimental coma —the one that preceded the twilight of our relationship— we spent almost two years fighting against an invisible enemy: time. Time in all its forms. Time that eroded us along the way; time that transformed us individually, making it difficult to recognize ourselves as us. But also the time we had run out of.

"I don't want you to be right," I said, surprising myself.

"Me neither, believe me, me either...," he answered.

There are people who have the mysterious ability to convey trust in just two sentences. He was one of them.

I had a revelation. I knew where I had seen that vaguely familiar face before. He was the same person who had sat behind me in FCC!

"Can I ask you one thing?" I said.

"Of course."

"That evening at the FCC, how could you guess what I was imagining?"

"Ah!" he exclaimed. "I knew it was you! You're the woman who spoke alone."

"What!? What do you mean? By no means do I speak alone."

"You do, you do... and you were doing it again right now when I arrived. But there is nothing wrong with that. In all fairness, it is not about talking alone, but with oneself. There are thoughts that simply shouldn't move from one side of the brain to the other. They need to come out first and then re-enter accompanied by fresh air. I wonder whether anyone has ever researched the issue, but—"

"Right, right...," I interrupted. "But I simply don't speak alone, or with myself, much less with strangers so...," I added while getting up.

"Don't go, please don't go," he replied.

"Give me one good reason why I shouldn't go."

"Because if you do, I will be the one who will be left talking alone... and I have so many things to tell you."

Again, your style came to mind.

"I'm not leaving. I just wanted to stand up to see the reflection of the moon over the river," I said as I discovered it was a new-moon night.

The stars reflected on the water, conveying the sensation that we were being enveloped by the universe. Only the hangover of a moving ship distorted the magical mirror the river had become. Fireflies, survivors of modern pesticides, fluttered over the deck as if some of those stars had detached from the sky. Macaques and other nocturnal creatures screamed from the jungle like wailing women, generating a surreal atmosphere in which the importance of our very existence diminished by the minute. After a few moments, without turning, I asked, "Are you still there?"

"No," he replied after a while.

The playful style reminded me of you again.

Then he added, "And speaking of time... Did you know that there are people who have a distorted perception of time? There are individuals who feel that time moves faster than it really does. They tend to achieve great things in life, perhaps because they live each day as if it were the last, although they also suffer more than most, perhaps because they feel death is approaching more quickly."

I was shocked! Those were the very same reflections that I had been writing about that morning. Once more, I felt that the stranger could read my mind.

"What are you doing on this ship?" I asked.

"I keep track of a ghost," he replied mysteriously.

"A ghost you say...," I answered.

"I'm tracing down a vapor, an ethereal substance, a mirage: love."

It reminded me of the last years of our relationship, when, on one occasion, you said to me, "Our essence has evaporated and there is nothing left but an empty bottle." And what did we do with that empty bottle? We put a message in it and threw it into the vast ocean of silence, instead of talking it through.

Inspired by his poetry, I decided to be poetic as well, "I think of love as one of those Russian dolls that fit into each other."

"Explain yourself," he said, inquisitively.

"I don't know... Sometimes, I feel as if the smallest of those dollies represents the first spark, the emergence of an electric falling in love. Then, time passes, and over that initial emotion another skin grows, that of loving, which is still passionate but less euphoric. And, then, more and more skins grow over each other, until that final layer resembles a warm wooly sweater: unattractive but necessary."

"I wish it was as you say. This way, one would always have the choice to descend to that first dolly, the core of love, and enjoy the cheerful laughter."

"The cheerful laughter?"

"Yes, the cheerful laughter. You fall in love because you laugh, and the more you laugh, the more you fall in love, I think it's the dopamine or some other chemical that connects both feelings. However, I have a vision of more… let's say evolutionist love. I think of the various phases of love as the larval stages of an insect, whereby one sentiment evolves into another, irreversibly."

"A pessimistic view," I replied.

"I'm not suggesting that the love butterfly completely flies away, but that that initial sentiment transforms into something else, neither better nor worse, just something else. But, besides, it was you, and not me, who instinctively conjectured that that old couple fervently kissing in the FCC was in fact married for the second time, instead of rejoicing in that latent love buried under layers and layers."

Difficult to admit but true. Thinking about our relationship, I didn't have much hope that that first dolly of love would still be alive, suffocated under all those other skins that we had grown over time. It is somehow devastating to conclude that love follows the very rules of thermodynamics, transforming itself from magical matter into useful matter. But who needs any more useful matter!? For that we already have wicker chairs, hinges for windows, and nacre letter openers. In life, we need magic; cheerful magic, wild magic, even useless but magical magic. It is difficult to come to terms with the fact that this clay of beautifully wet touch, with which we both played to model our most fantastic dreams, gradually dried up, becoming rigid, until irreparable cracks appeared.

I remember the day you said to me, "Maybe we should change our names, and that way we could get to know each other again." Those were the days when, in a rush, we crossed paths at airports to hand each other the house keys and remind the one heading home to water the plants. Afterward, and once on the plane, we would be silently grateful that we never got to kiss each other, because that way, when we see our relationship is about to enter a deep coma, we would kiss for the first time and we would revive the flame again. Unfortunately, though, sentimental death precipitated that rekindling.

I returned to my conversation with the stranger and asked, "And when you capture that ghost that you referred to —love— what do you plan to do with it?"

"I'm not aiming to capture it. I'm just trying to understand it. I'm documenting love stories that happened during the dark years of the Khmer Rouge."

I must confess that I didn't see either the transcendence or the relevance of such an activity.

"An innovative proposal," I responded, as if we were at a World Bank meeting.

"Innovative?" he replied with a grimace.

My lack of appreciation killed the moment a bit. Once more, I was disappointed with myself for having lost my past sensitivity for the small things. I blamed my profession, which had silently reprogrammed me to be clinical, objective, and rational; highly harmful elements for the instinct of love. However, when I later reconsidered that traveler's expedition, I not only saw it as relevant but also of social interest. If humanity had wasted centuries in the pursuit of useless treasures like gold coffers or fabulous gems, why not embark on the most pressing exploration: that of the soul. Love in modern times was becoming a coronary condition rather than a miracle.

When I finally decided to turn around to congratulate him on his initiative, the traveler was no longer there. In his chair, he had left the pages where I had written my most intimate reflections in the morning (which I had forgotten on the deck). Over my notes, he had added one of his own: "I haven't read it, and I won't read it again."

# CHAPTER FIVE

## MEKONG

I woke up at dawn in the middle of a vast ocean of fresh water, Tonle Sap Lake, a special lake that expands and contracts with the generous rains and the cruel drought—a bit like the heart does with love and unrequited love. I always found this lake unique, with its placid calm, timeless feeling, and voracious appetite that enables it to swallow the rice fields and villages at will in its expansion following the rains. Entire villages of floating houses (and lives struggling to stay afloat) live on its waters. People who are islands, or rather, lives that are islands. Would you feel like an inhabitant of Earth living here? I asked myself. It must be strange. It must be almost inhuman to live surrounded only by water, without land, even though we ourselves are also that: water. It must be like living surrounded by ourselves, an immense solitude.

At seven o'clock in the morning the hoarse trombone of the ship sounded, as if half apologizing for intruding on the locals' lives. We had reached one of the highlights of the cruise: the floating villages. For the next two hours, the inhabitants of the lake would become our circus show, and we would become theirs. The difference, perhaps, is that after those hours, some would set sail for their lives, whereas others would remain anchored in theirs. The waiters from the ship came and went, parading up and down along an improvised walkway connecting the floating village with the boat, smiling, loaded with trays and trays of exotic fish and multicolored fruits from mysterious lands. Trays and more trays, all of them blessed by rituals where the incense rose to heaven alongside the prayers.

The village's children, seen from above, joined their hands in a Buddhist sign of greeting; meanwhile, in a Christian act of compassion, the tourists threw coins at them. A child appeared, carrying a sack of what looked like rice, but which turned out to be toasted crickets. In an act of generosity, he began to throw handfuls of insects at the tourists to allow them to taste one of the most precious delicacies in the village. A fat woman who always brought a parasol with her, panicked when she saw herself covered in crickets, some of which had become entangled in her ringlets, and threw the parasol overboard while screaming uncontrollably. She gave such a powerful yell that her false teeth were projected overboard to sink to the bottom of the muddied waters.

The children reacted swiftly. They tied a rope to the youngest child's feet and, placing a weight around his neck, they threw him into the water, making sure he sank right to the bottom of the lake in search of the treasure. The tourists on deck, when they realized the atrocity of submerging a child with a chain wrapped around his neck, began to shout warnings at the children's parents, who didn't understand what the hell all the screaming was about when this was an innocent pastime for their children. After many attempts, all of them vigorously cheered by the young Cambodians while condemned in horror by the Westerners, the little amphibian was retrieved by his companions pulling on the rope, and there he was: emerging victorious, with fluorescent algae covering his hair, and his trophy shining in his hands. Everyone applauded, and just as the owner of the dentures began to catch her breath, the children started playing with the false teeth, putting them in their mouths, one by one, boasting with their white smiles. The poor woman again broke out in terrifying screams and fainted to the ground. She had to be assisted by the medical services on board.

Amid all that tumult, and as if taking advantage of the confusion, the mysterious man (who by then was a little less mysterious) made his way down the gangplank. He descended with astonishing determination to reach the square of that floating village. He first had to dodge one of the waiters on the gangplank, who juggled the tray he was using to carry more fish onboard, and then another officer dressed in immaculate white tried to make him understand that leaving the ship was contrary to protocol. The exchange was only fish for smiles, nothing more, and everyone should remain in their place. He was not persuaded. Instead, the man descended like a regal ox, with serene and firm steps, while holding his hands together in a Buddhist symbol of greeting, well above his forehead, in a clear sign of profound respect for that community. I realized that he knew the local symbology well. I couldn't help but feel admiration, followed by a feline curiosity.

Surrounded by a dozen children and adolescents, he exchanged greetings, indecipherable gestures, and several sentences with the locals, which triggered some very loud laughs. He tried the salted fish offered to him, and he even shared it with some of the children who followed his shadow. He didn't bother to look back to witness the shock generated among the ship's tourists, maybe because such an effect was too predictable or, as I discovered later, because he simply couldn't care less. I felt the burning desire to descend as well. The man continued chatting with those castaways of fate with absolute normality, and, after a few minutes of playing with the local children, he advanced across a rickety bridge that linked the handful of floating huts connected like a spider web and disappeared under the palm-leaf roofs. I imagined he had been escorted to the chief's house.

This was an unusual situation for me. I couldn't remember the last field operation during which I wasn't the chief of mission and, therefore, the one engaging with the local authorities first. I patiently waited for the tourist nebula to dissipate with the appearance of the pastries and breakfast, and then I jumped down the gangplank, determined to make it to the chief's house. When I opened the chief's door, upset with his excess of leadership, I was about to shout, "But who the hell do you think you are!" There he was: sitting on the floor, with his legs crossed one on top of the other, next to the chief, while the chief's wife was serving tea from a blue porcelain teapot, which was the only flash of color in the sober environment. Surprisingly, they were not staggered by my sudden intrusion. Instead, the mysterious man looked up from the notes he was taking, rearranged his round intellectual glasses, and, smiling, elegantly invited me to sit next to him without losing the thread of the conversation. The chief and his wife reacted with equal equanimity, perhaps believing that I was his wife, and simply late. I sat down, feeling naked without my laptop, or at least a notebook.

I focused on the ceremonious way in which the woman served tea. She seemed to have a young soul trapped in a body that had aged prematurely, marked by the wear and tear of living. But she had retained a lucid look and a gracious pair of hands. The man, kindly, shared with me some of his own notes, like a good colleague would do in a work meeting, and so I was able to quickly catch up on that surreal interview. Putting on my virtual bureaucrat's cap, I avidly scrutinized his indecipherable scribbles. Among all those pages, it struck me to read, "When did you know that you were really in love?"

"What!" I exclaimed, unrestrained.

The man noticed my surprise and whispered in my ear, "In this life you can ask whatever you want, as long as you smile," without a hint of pedantry and already transitioning to his next question to the chief.

It took me a few more questions to understand what the thread of the conversation was.

"Love in the time of the Khmer Rouge," the man said to me, noticing my clear gesture of incomprehension.

"Ah! Of course... love in the Khmer Rouge! But what a fool I was!" I said to myself with irony.

The man continued with his interview in relatively fluent Khmer, tinged with a strong French accent. I presumed he had resided in Cambodia at some point in his life, and he was probably related to the settlers of the old colony. I had to prick up my ears, as my command of Khmer was never optimal. But, assisted by the notes he kept passing on to me, I was able to derive that the conversation was some sort of walk through the past. I noticed that the chief would address the mysterious man as Lui; I deduced that his real name must be Louis. I finally found out his name! He was no longer so mysterious…

Louis asked brief questions, while the chief and his wife, Sopheara, responded with long digressions about the mystique of their love during the years of the genocide—love and genocide, two words that seldom come together in the same sentence. Louis, addressing Sopheara, asked with remarkable tenderness, "Ma'am, why did you decide to marry your husband, instead of Saroun?"

Sopheara shuddered and I, as a woman, could feel how she traveled back in time to that impossible bifurcation that she presumably revived every night in bed. Her husband looked down, perhaps because that very same past was also too heavy for him, or, maybe, full of fear of her imminent confession. Sopheara, with two drops of frosty dew on her eyes, replied, "Because my husband was good to Saroun, and I wanted to reward him with my eternal love," she said as she took her husband's hand.

Her husband, whom a life under the sun had endowed with the skin of an old elephant, kept looking at the floor while listening to the words she whispered for his benefit. He nodded, resigned, while shaking away tears as if they were unwelcome flies. "*Txa, txa...*" (yes, yes…) he kept repeating, while she tried to alleviate his visible pain, even his inexplicable feeling of guilt. I began to feel uncomfortable because of the emotional bloodshed Louis did not seem willing to stop.

"How did everything happen?" Louis asked.

"These people don't like to talk about that part of the past," I reproached him.

"These people…"? Louis responded, condescendingly, but sending me a clear message.

"I give you that," I said, apologizing for my paternalism. "But even so, Cambodians do not like to talk about those distant times."

He looked at me, smiling his indecipherable smile. I cursed people who always seem to be a step ahead of everyone else while managing to look adorable at the same time. He added, "I'm here because they asked me to come. They want to talk. Trust me."

Louis sorted out his notes while giving the couple time to sort themselves out, and then came back to the interrogation, "Madame, Sopheara," he said, calling her by her name, "would you like to tell us how everything unfolded?"

The woman took her husband's hand again and kissed it twice before letting it rest on the wooden floor. She seemed ready to open up to her interrogator. I mentally began to assemble the film reel and prepared myself for the cinematic release I sensed I was about to witness. When she began her narrative, I could almost hear the quiet rattle of the cinematograph.

Sopheara was born into a well-off family. Her father was a state official and her mother a high school teacher. She was the youngest of four sisters. Gifted in the arts from the start, she was born singing instead of crying. At the age of nine she confessed to her parents that she would recognize the love of her life when she made a man cry with her singing. The family interpreted that internal motivation as some divine sign and accepted that their daughter's destiny was nothing other but to sing as a magical giant ibis and ascend to heaven someday. Guided by the mystical strength of desire, she graduated from Cambodia's Royal University of Fine Arts. Her training did not take long to bear fruit. A stroke of fortune led her to perform in Paris during a rice festival. The Ministry of Agriculture sent a delegation of Cambodian businessmen to France, and she had the opportunity to dance for the president of the republic himself. Displaying long, ethereal fingers, like an *apsara,* and with the vibrant voice of young goldfinch she converted the white wine into a sparkling magic. Her piercing eyes, dark like the darkest nights, gobbled up everyone's gaze, and no nightingale could resist the fluttering of her wings. She was not yet twenty-three and still had a lifetime to dance.

Saroun, who was older than her, was the choreographer and representative of a dance company. All he knew, he had learned in the school of life. His fortuitous encounter with art began at the age of twelve, when each night he would make some money cleaning the cinema's seats of the remains of durian peels at the end of each show. Then, in the French postcolonial times, Phnom Penh was filled with theatres and cinemas and the city oozed culture. Without hesitation, he accepted a job behind the scenes as a handyman, which later on led to becoming an assistant director. Over the years he ended up learning the job of direction by watching thousands of staged shows, and as soon as he collected some money, he convinced his sister and two of his cousins that the future of the world was nothing but to dance and dance. Thus, the four threw themselves into the theater in a desperate adventure.

They were a small company with more ambition than talent, but with their perennial smiles and sparkling looks they managed to captivate all poor souls, which were many in those days. Chance led them to perform in front of King Norodom Sihanouk and his wife Queen Monineath, just before he had to go into exile after General Lol Nol's coup d'état. The coup happened at a family wedding in Takeo province, not far from Phnom Penh, where the king was in the midst of one of his many populist tours of the provinces, handing out greetings in exchange for flowers and support. It was a brief meeting, but the cameras were responsible for broadcasting their fortune all over the country.

It was then that Sopheara and Saroun met. She was playing *Lakhon luong* for the king's delight and under the mesmerized eyes of hundreds of people. It was a night with a shy breeze and yellowish moon, a night on which the world seemed different, and so did life. The clangorous croaking of the swamp reminded those in attendance that life is little more than mud, and destiny clay to be shaped. And then it happened that, in the midst of all that silent poetry, Sopheara improvised a fabulous lyric unwritten in the script. Sometimes it happened. Her voice was hijacked by deities from other worlds, and she would begin to sing with a supernatural resonance while her eyes would turn from the deepest black to the pristine blue waters of Ilha de Sete Paos. Saroun, sitting in the audience, became stranded in time by that everlasting voice. Perhaps reminded of when his mother used to sing him that song as a lullaby, or maybe spellbound by the magical aura that surrounded Sopheara, he simply stood up, took the *troche* by the stage, and, sitting slightly behind her, accompanied her celestial voice with the instrument. At the end of the song, she turned to contemplate what she had already sensed: Saroun's weeping. He had become the man of her life.

Saroun's theater company experienced a brief period of glory with Sopheara onboard. She brought in all her creativity and magic. They soon began to present their own works that dazzled the audience, transporting them to dreamy realities. They performed in almost all the theaters and nightclubs of Phnom Penh, as well as in other important cities in the country, such as Siem Reap, Kep, and Kampot. They even traveled to the mystical city of Vientiane, in Laos, and to the former capital of Myanmar, Mandalay, where the country's authorities greeted them with a shower of golden padauk flowers and a river cruise back to Rangoon, which Saroun and Sopheara would always remember as the honeymoon they never had.

There are lives that are lived condensed in just a few moments. Theirs was one of them. Sopheara, with her graceful and delicate dances, captivated half of rural Cambodia. There, among the rice fields, was where she would be complete and where her dances became ethereal and sublime. She would transform into pure nature, and her voice vibrated with such intensity that it would make the coconuts fall from the palm trees and trigger the flight of strange birds that inexplicably began mating in the air. Saroun —born of mud and natural elements— knew that this was the power of nature being expressed through her. For that reason, he liked to organize functions in the most unlikely places, arranging floating sets on rivers or marshes, or decorating the pre-Angkorian ruins of Preah Vihear with an infinite number of candles so that she could dance feeling like what she was: a Goddess from the past.

But on April 17, 1975, shadows spread over the Kingdom of Cambodia. The Khmer Rouge guerrillas finally reached the capital and, street by street, the shouting men in black ordered the complete evacuation of Phnom Penh under the pretext that American B-52s were about to bomb it. Even the terminally ill were literally dragged out of hospitals on stretchers and pulled along the cobblestones to a certain death, only elsewhere. It was like emptying a huge pumpkin until only the skin remained. That macabre day the whole country retreated several centuries into the darkness of the Middle Ages, and the country once known as the Pearl of Asia was swallowed by a huge black oyster.

Saroun and Sopheara, who had performed the previous afternoon at the Preah Suramarit National Theater, were surprised by the soldiers on a rooftop, naked, after having spent the night making love under the stars. At bayonet point —showing their sulfurous teeth in laughter— the guerillas pushed them onto the street where, still dressing each other, they wandered without knowing what the hell was going on. They wandered for days, sometimes on foot, at other times in an oxcart, and with only two suitcases loaded with their makeup and theatre outfits, which they would never wear again. It was a parade of thousands of broken, lost souls stumbling ghost-like in the same direction: death. Finally, Saroun and Sopheara arrived at the province of Battanbang, where both had family, or still so believed; however, at the gates of glory, they were made prisoners by militiamen of the Angkar, the Communist Party of Cambodia.

The soldiers who searched their suitcases had no doubt that they were putrid intellectuals, and therefore had to be re-educated. Sent to a forced labor camp, near Tonle Sap Lake, the couple were given the same task as several million other Cambodians: dig and dig long irrigation canals, for fourteen hours a day, dogged by the rapacious looks of their crypt keepers and tortured by the constant memory of the last breaths of those executed under the palm trees.

Life in the countryside was hell on Earth. Saroun and Sopheara could only see each other in the distance, both digging in their own mud, in their own solitude, just like all the other hundreds of souls in the concentration camp. And yet they found comfort in knowing they were both alive. They slept in separate shacks, although they would always meet in their dreams, dressed in their fancy costumes, like when they used to act on stage. She would wear long, kittenish eyelashes, and he would present himself dressed in his best outfit from infancy: innocence. Every night they dreamed the same dreams. Saroun arrived riding on his black horse, dressed as a pre-Angkorian warrior, and she would ride on horseback, feeling safe as a princess, far away from that nightmare and in the direction of paradise. There was no dream more desired than to see the end of that absurd genocide.

However, by the morning, the dream would evaporate in the pond, where they continued contemplating each other in the distance, discreetly, to avoid attracting the attention of their custodians, using their pick or shovel, carrying mud from one place to another with their own bare hands in an archaic attempt to build an irrigation channel to nowhere. They would beam their energy and hope to each other when they noticed that the other was succumbing to despair, which was often, and they would dry each other's tears by blowing in the wind when they felt like crying, which was always.

Carnal love would find its way once a month. That was on new moon nights, when Saroun furtively crawled through the mud to Sopheara's hut to quench his thirst in her intimate well, often filled with more tears than love. She would be kind to him, using a moistened rag to tenderly wash away the mud on him, to leave his skin in the state of grace like that of a newborn. He ran his fingertips all over her body, while she ignored the sandpaper of his touch and imagined the tenderness of his loving intentions. In that tiny palm-leaf room, the sound of breath had nowhere to hide, and the music of their hearts felt like two distant drums. Two naked bodies and a common desire: the ultimate expression of love.

He, in absolute silence to avoid discovery, would indicate with his fingers the number of the song that should sound in their minds, and, she, transported into the past, would remember when Saroun used to do just that from behind the curtain to remind her what act was coming next. Glorious music would then ooze from within, making each organ resonate and each inch of skin tremble, and releasing each imprisoned memory. Making the music sound in their minds was the only way to listen to music in a world in which any form of culture had simply perished. Afterward, they would lie together and emulate penetration; however, they felt only frustration, as it is well known that the sexual instinct is the first to be repressed in captivity, since love is and must always feel free. They would then say goodbye among disconsolate tears, having to wait for twenty-eight more nights until the next new moon.

Surviving the concentration camp was not a matter of effort, but of pure chance. Each afternoon, after the meager ration of fish water —known as ghost soup— the camp guard allowed half an hour of rest on the mud. It was the most agonizing half hour any human being could endure. Meantime, the guard would go to sleep on a reed mat under a palm tree. That half hour passed with the anticipation of imminent executions. When he awoke, the guard methodically lit a cigarette and began to walk among the ditches where the prisoners waited in the most unimaginable, mournful silence. Neither the cicadas nor birds dared make a sound. The silence was overwhelming. The only sound the prisoners noticed was the beating of hundreds of stony hearts that threatened to escape from their chests.

The guard would begin his walk with the ceremonial parsimony of a divine entity that controls life, with the power to give it or take it away. He saw the prisoners as soulless carcasses, as people who had ceased existing, which was somewhat true. He always hummed a song in a low voice while he walked. And, when his cigarette only had one puff left, the guard offered it to the prisoner closest to him, and, while the unfortunate person gave his or her last shaky breath, the guard drew his weapon and mercilessly put a bullet in one eye. The guard would not distinguish between man or woman, boy or girl. The smell of tobacco mingled with the scent of gunpowder, and the mud turned a strange ruby color.

It was a matter of faith. Sooner or later that regime, as sadistic as it was absurd, would collapse; everything would return to normal, and life would return to what it once had been—a dance. It was a matter of time, because no harm lasts a hundred years. But Sopheara fell ill with an infection in one foot, the result of a badly healed wound she had sustained while digging in the irrigation channels. The high fever at night would not let her rest, and Saroun feared that the guards would view her as weak and would invite her to smoke among the mallows. The fevers did not abate, and the infection was spreading like a caterpillar all along her calf, which had turned a gangrenous purple color. Saroun, in the absence of nursing or medical care, crawled every night to the lake to collect medicinal plants with which to make a poultice of love and herbs. After two months of putting his life at stake, in one of those raids of desperate love, he was discovered by the guards, who believed he intended to steal food from the kitchen.

The guards took Saroun to the camp commander. The commander didn't even bother asking what the charges were. Instead, he opened his big mouth, and his bleeding gums dictated Saroun's sentence. The commander then put his hand into his pocket to try to find a cigarette. But he had run out. And, for some strange reason, the executioner concluded that he couldn't kill without smoking. He cursed himself for smoking his last cigarette with no purpose before going to bed. He barked like a rabid dog, ordering the prisoner to be taken to the "palm tree of last sighs" and there to be beheaded immediately. The guard ordered to behead Saroun happened to be the chief of the floating village, Sopheara's husband. Surprisingly, he had volunteered to execute the mission. Thus, at dawn, Saroun was escorted, handcuffed, to the fateful palm tree. Sopheara and Saroun would never see each other again.

The interviewer, after hearing the story, became silent, and his perennial smile had disappeared from his lips. He looked back and forth between Sopheara and her husband, searching for something to say. He stuttered like a novice sacristan.

"He is a good man," Sopheara repeated while she held her husband's hand.

The chief fixed his eyes again on a small hole in the wooden floor, where they remained as he contemplated the stagnant past, which seemed to be floating above the floor. Louis, meanwhile, kept on looking at him judgmentally. A tense silence spread through the room.

"But…? I don't understand… Why…?" Louis stuttered, not knowing how to formulate the obvious question: how could she possibly marry the man who executed the love of her life?

Knowing Louis would fail to articulate the question given his emotional state, I tried: "Madame, what did your husband do to earn your love?"

Sopheara didn't hesitate for even half a second: "My husband immortalized my love for Saroun."

Louis and I looked at each other uncomprehendingly, while Sopheara and her husband looked at each other in mutual understanding. Two such different worlds were colliding under that palm roof. Sopheara sobbed before explaining the rest of the story.

"My husband didn't execute Saroun as he was ordered to do," she said in a somewhat questioning tone as she looked at her husband. "Instead, he risked his own life by letting Saroun escape. After the apparent execution, my husband returned to the camp and explained to his superiors that he had slaughtered the criminal and thrown his body into the river. He put his own life at risk for me and took care of me for the rest of my captivity. I am indebted to him. Over time, I came to know that my husband had been in love with me since the day I arrived at the concentration camp. And he also knew of my love for Saroun, as well as our nocturnal escapades. But he never gave us away. He remained there, in the shade, resigned, craving to be the recipient of my love. When Saroun managed to escape with his help, my future husband took great care that I did not lack anything. He got the medicines that I needed to heal my wound; he provided me with boiled rice at night in my hut, and when that cruel guard prowled near me, with his death cigarette dangling from his lips, he always found a way to lead him somewhere else on some pretext."

Louis and I listened to the story, stunned, shocked, and even with some disbelief. We could have remained there for hours, asking hundreds of questions to better comprehend the mysteries of that reality so alien to ourselves. Our impulse was to ask her if she ever tried looking for Saroun after the war ended; how she could go about her daily life, knowing her lost love might be searching for her on every hill, on every reef, in every shadow. We would have liked to ask her whether she was happy, there in the middle of that vast lake of solitude. But our world was, perhaps unfortunately, too complex, while theirs was, perhaps luckily, somewhat simpler.

Thus, acknowledging that the ways of the Lord are inscrutable and the divine design an unfathomable mystery, we ended the encounter by thanking them for their time, taking a picture together —in which we all had our eyes closed— and leaving. When Sopheara stood up, I could see in her silhouette the spike of the late wheat, and in her golden aura the shadow of the ethereal dancer she once was. We left behind a man relieved because that obscure chapter was closing again, and a woman, somewhat less joyful, because that same chapter filled with doubts had been reopened. Her farewell to me was unexpected. While hugging me, she whispered in my ear, "Thank you for not asking what you had on your mind."

When we crossed the gangplank, going back to our flagship, Louis didn't delay asking me the same question I used to ask my father at the end of every Alfred Hitchcock film: "Do you think he was the murderer?"

And I gave him the same answer my father used to give me: "Only the murderer and the victim know that."

Upon reaching the deck, still immersed in the chloroform of that acrid dream, we unconsciously floated up to two wicker armchairs overlooking the immensity of the lake. We stayed there, submerged in a sonorous silence and for an indefinite time, each one processing the information as best we could. I couldn't stop thinking that on that floating island an imprisoned siren lived. Still today, I feel the driving need to get on the first plane bound for Cambodia, paddle to that floating jail of sticks, and free the siren from her destiny. And I think that if I don't finally take that plane, it's because I empathize with her and with the fear of being liberated, having to manage the excess of freedom once released. Sometimes we are more prisoners of ourselves than of life per se.

After a prolonged silence, I asked Louis what my mother used to ask my father when he spent more than two minutes in silence: "What are you thinking?"

Louis responded like a proper man: "Nothing."

"But you must be thinking something," I replied.

Louis smiled. "I really wasn't thinking anything. But since you're asking, last night, after our conversation, I thought that this jazz that life is would perhaps sound more cheerful and varied if there were several short melodies in it, instead of just a long one."

"I see…" I answered. "I think *nothing* was a better answer."

"Why?" Louis asked, surprised.

"Because I can imagine the thought that must have crossed your mind: and what if this woman were one of my multiple melodies…"

"Wouldn't you like to sound for me?" Louis asked, smiling.

"And know I'm one more song in your long serenade? No thanks. Also, how can you be thinking about all that after the story we just heard about that sad dancer?" I said.

"I already told you that just now I wasn't thinking anything! This is something that occurred to me last night," he replied, gesturing comically. "In any case, that wasn't how my analogy was intended to sound; I just think that even the most beautiful love song ultimately loses its charm every time you listen to it."

"I respectfully disagree," I answered. "I think of a song as an enigma, as an intrigue that leads straight to the heart. At the beginning you listen only to its lyrics and melody, and soon you make the mistake of believing you've already heard everything. But behind those simple rhymes, fabulous verses can be hidden. And beyond that diaphanous melody you can find hidden harmonics, which must be deciphered little by little, with the symphonic step of a lifetime, with a sunset, under rain, on this very ship, making that music always sound like a new song."

The ship gave the sad bellow of a titan, and the propellers began to churn the waters, enveloping the floating people in whirlpools that gradually regained their peace. From the floating platform, the whole village waved their hands in farewell, while on board the tourists delighted themselves with huge crab legs with Kampot pepper, throwing the crabs' skeletons into the water with impunity.

Louis smiled, aloofly, silently, and I couldn't resist asking again, "What are you thinking now? And don't say *nothing*."

"No, now I was thinking of something, as a matter of fact..." he answered. "Hypothetically, and only hypothetically, I was wondering what that song you described before would sound like if we listened to it together."

"That would be just a fantasy," I answered bluntly.

Louis wrapped himself in a strange silence, and I quickly realized that I must have said something wrong.

"A fantasy?" he replied tersely. "Let me think... what's fantasy? That woman, Sopheara, lived two years of her youth wrapped in, as we would describe it, a fantasy. In that fantasy, she dressed in golden clothes and was adorned with fictional tiaras, dancing on celestial stage after stage and next to a love also born out of a fairy tale. I wonder: was that fantasy less real than her present, anchored to a piece of floating bamboo? Presumably, that past fantasy became the very essence of her life, if not life itself, and that 'fantasy' is probably the only thing that prevents her from sinking into the deep shadows of these waters.

"I've always wondered why people make such an effort to present fantasy as the antithesis of reality, as a lie, as something false. Fantasy... I think of fantasy as an essential part of life, as a dimension as real as what we like to call reality, but where we can be more free to alter the fundamental parameters to experience wonderful things; where we have all the editorial rights on the novel of our own life; where we can stop being who we pretend to be, to be truly ourselves," said Louis. He paused for a few seconds before continuing with his impassioned speech.

"And, the same with love. Why would a fleeting voyage on this ship be a fantasy? One can live the most extraordinary love story in just three unforgettable days and then spend a lifetime treasuring those memories, even making them evolve, hosted in the subconscious. Speaking again hypothetically, and only hypothetically, I think that whatever you and I decided to live aboard this firefly ship would be as real as life itself and that emotion would only become an illusion if one of us suddenly stopped to believe in it."

Louis spoke with such conviction about his own beliefs that I panicked. I unexpectedly had an overwhelming sense of déjà vu as I remembered that evening in the past when I met you. That hypnotizing personality was too familiar to me, and I knew I had to decide quickly between fleeing in time or staying forever. That first afternoon, walking through the streets of Oxford, I was about to run when I met you. Fortunately, I did not.

After a calm pause, Louis concluded, "Some time ago, I chose to live swathed in fantasy. In the end, when the black crow comes to fetch me, others may decide on my behalf if my life was a pure fantasy or purely fantastic."

# CHAPTER SIX

## PART THREE: MEKONG

The third day on the peaceful waters dawned calmly. Listening to Vivaldi enticed me to do some reading on the deck, where, warmed by sunbeams, I was ultimately lulled into that poetic trance where fiction and reality merge. The night, however, took on a different nature: a chardonnay downpour, served in wide glasses, unleashed an internal thunderstorm, just like when I was young.

Since the experience in the floating village, an old theme —love— felt very present in my reflections. I spent the whole afternoon clinging to my favorite novel, which I must have read about thirteen times and which I usually carry religiously with me on any work mission, as an exorcizing bible to combat the negative externalities of my job. I thought of Saroun as the main character of that novel of unrequited love. My cruise aboard that fluvial ship, impeccable like that of the novel set in the Caribbean, served as a perfect shuttle between the two parallel stories. I wondered if Sopheara, the captive dancer, lived with the same hopes of seeing Saroun appear one day on board one of those ships. But what if that were the case? What if it really happened that Saroun broke into her life again? Would he, would she, would both be happier that way?

Would she feel more in love in that physical relationship, inevitably perishable, than with his memory, inevitably magical? That has remained my circular thought since you left.

That was the day of the gala dinner on board. The captain, properly dressed for the occasion, would grace us with his presence in the dining room. I wasn't particularly excited at the thought of being surrounded by dozens of withered roses and their usual conversations about multicolored pills, but the alternative of checking my email in my room wasn't exactly an invitation to joy either. I was drying my hair after a warm shower when I heard a subtle sound under the door. I opened it without delay, forgetting that I was wrapped in a towel, displaying myself as a happy mummy. It was my new friend Louis. On one knee, and with his ear against the floor, I caught him by surprise while slipping something under my door. Never before had I seen anyone blush like that. He looked like one of those wild mushrooms that warn of their danger.

"Ships' doors always leave a good gap with the floor, of about two centimeters, so that swelling of the wood doesn't block the door," he said, improvising. "But not this one," he added.

I crackled, and the towel loosened, almost falling to the ground. I quickly recomposed myself and then noticed that Louis had an envelope in his hand. I imagined it was an invitation to dinner that he had tried to slide under the door. I couldn't comprehend, though, why he wasn't simply asking me, as modern people do aboard old ships. But I interpreted it as one more French eccentricity, and I tore the letter out of his hands while he was still on one knee as though he was proposing. I swiftly pronounced a spontaneous "I do," surprising myself.

"Just give me a few minutes to change, and I'll join you at dinner," I added smiling.

Louis's face showed his tremendous surprise, which I attributed to a post-traumatic effect. He stammered, "Yes, yes… dinner… yes… It will be fun!" while rushing along the narrow corridor.

"It will be fun" made him sound like a teenager inviting his date to the prom instead of the impetuous man he was. I closed the door and opened the envelope in a rush, acting like an excited adolescent myself. It contained four pages, covered with his handwriting on both sides. It seemed to be a narrative version of Sopheara's story. I couldn't finish reading it before dinner, but the first paragraphs had a literary quality that was more than acceptable. Perhaps it had one or two adjectives more than necessary, maybe fewer commas than good English grammar demanded, but, generally, the text flowed well and with a magical realism unusual for Cambodian characters. His description of Sopheara's gaze was particularly striking: "…behind those eyes as dark as withered happiness lived the glimpse of a spark; the suspicion of a door that, perhaps, hid a long corridor winding toward another sincerer form of happiness, where her dancing was still joyful and her singing artful."

After reading the first pages, an irrational sense of envy seized me for a moment. I wanted to write like that again! There was a time when writing prose was my favorite hobby, especially during ocher autumns and warm rainy days. But over time (time, again), everything that wasn't profitable or useful had become extinct. Those damn official reports that force a person to eradicate each adjective until full asepsis is achieved...

Once I recovered from my attack of childish jealousy, another instinct, this one even more basic, came to me: that of conquest. I dressed in my most seductive garment: a gauzy black dress, accented by a subtle white motif, which left my shoulders dangerously exposed. I put up my hair with a nacre clip I had bought in Delos. I applied some subtle makeup —trying not to disguise my maturity— and adorned myself with my long earrings from India, whose mysterious design used to attract my dates, who would come closer, taking away with them the scent of my Estée Lauder perfume as a gift.

When I arrived at the restaurant, I found Louis sitting near the bar. When he saw me, he immediately complimented me: "Those eyes match the earrings very well," he said while approaching. "Hmmm, don't tell me: *Pleasures* is the name of your perfume... am I right?"

I couldn't help smiling. "How did you guess?"

The lounge was ready for us. The subdued lighting evoked the mysticism of a holy temple, the wide wineglasses emanated the spirits of wine, and the slight swaying of the ship reminded us that life is an eternal indecipherable trembling.

"Two margaritas, please," Louis asked the waiter.

"How do you know I want a margarita?"

"I didn't know," he replied, smiling.

As I took my cocktail, I noticed the inexplicably sharp gaze of a young lady in her late thirties. She was sitting alone at a table set for two. She wore a seductive green dress that reminded me of the emeralds of Boyacá. She kept staring at Louis and me. I wanted to ask Louis if he knew that attractive woman, but I didn't because I feared he would suddenly turn around, revealing that I had been watching her too.

"By the way, I've flipped through your report— Sorry! Your writing!" I said, cursing myself for not timing my observation for a better moment in the evening.

Louis smiled intuitively.

"Aha! And... you liked my report?" he asked sarcastically.

"Well... I'm not sure, you see... The message is somewhat unclear—"

"You can relax," Louis interrupted bluntly.

"Excuse me?" I replied, irritated.

"I'm saying that you can relax. With me, and here, you can relax. You're not in D.C." he said.

The words of an old friend of mine, also a writer, came to mind: "We writers write to make others fall in love, not to transmit; compliment us by saying how you felt, not what you've understood." Buying time, I sipped my margarita, dragging my lips over the frosty sugar on the rim, as if trying to neutralize the bitter comment I would have made under normal circumstances. But by that point in the soiree, I had already resolved how I wanted the evening to end, and I didn't want to change my own plans, let alone compromise the success of an ongoing operation.

"I thoroughly appreciate your kind invitation to relax," I said.

My words were acceptable, but my feline gesture was unconvincing. Louis took his glass by the stem, examined me closely, and said, "That is what the Bank does to you: it chews you up and then spits you out."

Disconcerted, I hesitated. "Excuse me, do we know each other?"

"Ninth floor, right?" he asked. I nodded. "Seventh floor, Governance," he added.

"Do you work for the Bank, too?" I asked, curious.

"Now only at times."

"Short-term assignments?"

"Yes."

"But have our paths crossed before?" I asked, trying to remember.

"For several years, almost daily, in that cold steel lift. You used to wear linen dresses in the warm months and, in winter, turtleneck that clung to my own throat. Always with bright yellow trainers, which I imagine you would exchange for heels once in your office. More than once I wanted to warn you against those awful turtlenecks, and if I didn't, it was not out of fear to offend you, but because of that excessive code of conduct that human resources made us all sign to prevent sexual harassment. That was the end of all spontaneity…"

"Of sexist jokes, you mean." His inappropriate comment made me laugh. And, although I didn't admit it, there was some truth in his words: that subscription to American corporate values created a completely sterile environment.

"You know such a comment would be utterly inappropriate at headquarters," I said, smiling.

"Precisely! That's why I waited for years to say so on board this damn ship. Cheers!" he toasted, raising his glass.

Louis emptied his glass in one gulp, not very elegantly, and asked for two more of the same.

"By the way, congratulations on your new position as practice manager," said Louis.

"Am I under surveillance?" I asked playfully.

Louis grimaced like an old fox.

"With those yellow sports shoes... how could I possibly forget you?"

I smiled at his risky observation, and the conversation gained a few extra inches of trust.

"What's your specialty within Governance?"

"A bit of everything, and a lot of nothing, but mainly I worked on corruption and the positive spillovers on macroeconomic growth," Louis explained unenthusiastically.

"Hold on a second... Are you Louis Lemière? The one who, a few years ago, wrote the most controversial report ever about how, in some countries, high corruption indexes lead, paradoxically, to economic development?"

"Yes. I'm afraid so," he replied with false humility.

"But you were sector director until recently..."

"Exactly: *I was*. Until I resigned. Can we talk about something else? How about love, women, and life?"

"Do not invoke Mario Benedetti in vain," I said, making it clear that I was not ignorant about poetry. "But I don't get it... And what is all this about the interview with that family in the floating village?"

"What don't you get?" he replied.

"That you are..." I started, leaving the sentence suspended.

"That I am...?" he asked, inviting me to finish it, to fall into my own trap.

"Well... that that is a highly regarded position, one of those that anyone would aspire to."

"Correct. And to that position I consecrated a big chunk of my life until I realized that I was becoming one more cog in the factory."

"I see... because those of us who work on weekends to change the world are all a bunch of morons, right?"

"I haven't said that. It's a personal choice," he said, with little devotion and no conviction.

"But that's what you're thinking…"

Louis fixed his eyes on the ice in his glass, as if he himself was floating on one of those tiny icebergs.

"Tell me one thing," he said solemnly. "To what extent is what you do about development and not about yourself?"

I knew the answer, and it wasn't that I didn't want to confess it to him; rather, I didn't want to confess it to myself.

"I've had this conversation before," I said. "There seems to be a whole new kind of hippie trend within the institution, whose sole purpose seems to be making the rest feel guilty."

Louis realized that he was losing me, and, perhaps reminding himself that he had also resolved how he wished the evening to end, radically changed his strategy: "You are not at the Bank, Gipani, and, fortunately, no turtleneck suffocates your elegant heron's neck."

He caught me by surprise. It was my turn to blush like one of those poisonous mushrooms strewn throughout the Nordic forests.

"Tell me: how do you guys do it?" I asked, obviously flattered. "Is it the Latin genes?"

Louis smiled. "It isn't clear."

"What isn't clear?" I asked.

"It isn't clear whether the French qualify as Latin or not. We like to think so, but then the Spaniards and the Italians came and conquered the Mediterranean just for themselves."

A young local waiter, whose uniform resembled a carnival costume, accompanied us to our table at the semi-open end of the dining room, near where the other young woman had kept us under watch. Everything was in perfect order over the calm river waters: the virgin white tablecloth, the twinkling bluish candle at its center, the solid sparkling cutlery. The new breeze brought fresh conversation topics.

"So, you became a writer?" I asked rhetorically.

Louis interpreted my words with caution, not knowing whether I was taking him seriously or not. I anticipated that and rushed to add, "There was a time when I also wanted to be a writer, you know?"

He relaxed, without fully lowering his defenses. I realized that his writing was presumably a new occupation in which he might not feel fully established yet. I felt touched by his apparent vulnerability.

"Tell me about that furtive activity of yours," he said while resting his broad back against the wicker chair.

"Nothing serious. I never went beyond short stories written on the back of my university notes during insomniac nights. Free thoughts and poorly concatenated verses, mostly."

"But isn't that what writing is all about? And when you finally find a few pages that are relatively decipherable for the rest of the mortals, you send them to a publisher and wait, and wait, just like when throwing a message in a bottle," Louis said.

"Tell me more about that interview with Sopheara. What did you do that for?" I asked.

"It's the substrate for the novel I'm working on now. It's about love during the Khmer Rouge regime. I'm interested to know how the most beautiful flowers manage to flourish even in the dung."

"I was surprised to see you descending the gangplank with such determination. How did you know that Sopheara lived there?"

Louis got distracted when we passed by a mangrove redoubt on which millions of multicolored fireflies fought for space over the treetops.

"They're like Christmas trees," said Louis with childlike awe, revealing his innermost layer.

"Louis? My question, can you answer my question, please?" I demanded.

"It's a secret," he answered solemnly. "But for being you..." he added in a flattering tone and with one of his characteristic smiles. "One of the instructor judges of the court for the Cambodian genocide is a good friend of mine, and very Argentinian as well. He shared with me the transcripts from some of the witnesses in the famous case against Kang Kek, alias Duch."

"Have you read the files?" I asked.

"Only a fraction of the literally millions of pages of overwhelming stories of that systematic killing machine. But among those chilling passages fantastic stories are also hidden, such as that of Sopheara. I find it most enjoyable to realize that the purest forms of love are precisely born during the harshest times."

Louis fixed his gaze again on the fireflies that still adorned the river shore like stars fallen from the sky. I rescued him from there by saying, "I have a friend, a writer too, who always insists that writers write to make people fall in love. Is that your motive as well?"

Louis suddenly adopted a different stance. "I don't. I write to reach places that I can't reach myself."

Fortunately, the ordered chardonnay arrived at that precise moment, giving me enough time to digest his cryptic message.

"I can't comprehend what it is that someone who became sector director couldn't reach." I was unimpressed with myself for having mixed work with pleasure.

Louis laughed with that Frenchified mannerism that I would have detested had it not to come from him. He took shelter again in a few seconds of mystical reflection while reading the back label of the bottle, and then answered, "Love, for example?"

I wasn't expecting such an answer after only the second glass of wine. "Love?" I asked.

"I'm still a virgin," he said, without smiling.

For some strange reason, the thought of a man losing his virginity was difficult to reconcile. I always assumed that men came already deflowered, or something like that, which of course was an absurd physiologically and even more so sentimentally. Louis smiled. "It's inconceivable, isn't it?"

I wanted to answer with a resounding yes, but it didn't seem strategic to agree so easily, especially if he was simply playing with words. I responded in World Bank fashion: "It requires some thinking about."

Louis changed the topic. "Tell me, what brings you to Cambodia?"

I noticed then that the attractive woman, seated two tables away and still sitting alone, continued to stare at us conspicuously. Louis had his back to her. I wanted to warn him of the situation, but I feared that his French impetus would cause him to react disproportionately and all this would end in a cat fight. I ignored it again.

"I'm on a mission," I answered, without much imagination.

"On board this ship?" he asked. "Are you spying on someone?"

Had he noticed that I was looking at that woman? I wondered. Damn Louis and his ambiguous statements! That was precisely why I didn't like to date writers. They were always playing with metaphors.

"I came for the end of the fiscal year and to review some analytical products in our portfolio," I answered like an automaton. "But please, explain what all this is about losing your virginity. Because you are not a virgin, even remotely…"

Louis let out a roar of laughter that made the older couple to our left squirm uncomfortably in their seats, as if their hearing aids had blown.

"And don't dare touch the glass until you've confessed the truth!" I added, pointing at him with the tip of my fork.

Louis placed the glass on the table, and putting his hands up in mock surrender, said, "I am! I confess, I am! Regarding chronic love, I am still a virgin."

"What's all this about chronic love? Come on, answer, you damn writer! And don't you dare replying using adjectives or allegories!" I said, bringing the fork closer to his neck.

I was having a pleasant time. Away from my daily obsessions and routines, I was even starting to recognize myself. It had been a while since I was in front of someone and ready to, symbolically at least, comfortably undress myself.

"May I?" he asked, again drinking his wine in one gulp. "You see... for me there are two types of love: the one that lives for a few months, and the one that dies over a lifetime."

"A tragic description of love," I said, "but go on."

"Do you have empirical evidence that contradicts what I'm saying?"

"Maybe. Go on."

"I can't live without feeling permanently in love. I'm addicted to that state of mind and soul," Louis said simply, reducing the intensity of his words with one of his incorrigible smiles.

"What do you mean by that? Come on! Leave the hieroglyphics for the Egyptians and talk to me as the sector director that you once were!" I exclaimed.

Louis seemed to enjoy seeing this practice manager —whom he had presumably judged as uptight and of one single annual orgasm— acting like a fishwife.

He replied, "Mainly ephemeral sentiments: the first exchange of furtive glances, the first undiagnosed arrhythmia, the first evening floating over a fresh conversation, the first dance where you seem to feel a hasty kiss in your neck while doubting whether it really happened, the intense fear of unrequited love... All fragile sensations, transient and perishable, but also extraordinary, intoxicating, and addictive. Yes! I'm indeed addicted to that chimerical emotion, to that chemical reaction, to that magical sensation —sometimes regardless of the woman that triggers it all."

As Louis was finishing his speech, the fierce-looking woman who had been watching us all night passed very close to our table as she was leaving the restaurant and deliberately hit Louis' head with her purse. However, Louis didn't even flinch and continued talking about his encounters with life instead.

"What was that!?" I said, alarmed.

"What do you mean?" he replied, with extraordinary self-control.

"What do I mean? That woman just passed by your side and intentionally hit you with her purse!"

"You think so? She might have been dizzy with the swaying of the waves."

"What swaying? It couldn't be calmer."

"Maybe she drank a bit too much," he said, filling my glass impassively. "Drink some more wine."

I couldn't understand it. That woman had clearly hit him hard on the head with her purse. It was physically impossible that he noticed nothing. But he seemed so calm. Maybe it was the alcohol. I shrugged off that surreal incident and dived back into the charming soiree.

Louis had a curious way of perceiving love, or what he understood by it. However, I couldn't agree with his definition of love. His view of that wonderful sensation was too ephemeral in itself; too tragic, too argumentative about the very death of that fantastic spring in which that "I will always love you" actually blooms. No. I could not and did not want to subscribe to that vision of the world in which loving someone until the end meant losing the spell halfway; although, to tell the truth, I couldn't reject his conception based on my own example.

"Do you live, or have you ever lived, with someone?" I asked.

"What did I just explain?" he replied.

"You'll be left alone in life," I said, sounding extremely patronizing.

"None of that!" he said theatrically. "In fact, my greatest dream is to know that all the women who have ever fallen in love with me will attend my wake. And with no hard feelings. Yes! Especially that: no hard feelings, which might be more even more difficult to achieve than having all of them come."

Had I not known the rigorous professional development and career advancement required to reach the position of sector director, I would have labeled Louis as an eccentric. However, I decided to lend some credence to his words or, at least, to be amused with his divergent vision of that coronary disease called *love*.

"I presume it will be a small funeral. A dozen beloved women, maybe?" I said.

"Not beloved, in love," he remarked. "And it might be a bit more than just a dozen."

"Twenty?"

"Some more." He tried to look modest.

"Fifty!?"

Louis apologetically gestured that I should increase that figure. I couldn't believe I was questioning him like this about his love life.

"One hundred?" I exclaimed.

Again, that gesture of his, as if apologizing for his lack of romantic restraint.

"One hundred and fifty!?"

"Let's leave it at a few, okay?" he rushed to answer. "And that would include my sister, my dear mother, and my aunt Juliette, with whom I also fell in love, albeit in a very different way, of course," he added, smiling.

We let the evening, like the ship, take its course. The fireflies grew in number by the minute and became increasingly playful, just like us. The wine turned sparkling and finally developed a supernatural effervescence. The night was fresh and joyful, and a mysterious tingling had already begun to creep up my calves toward the center of the universe. Sulfurous bubbles emerged from the bottom of the river, which, with the churning of the propellers, left a yellowish fluorescent trail over the waters. While looking at that mysterious natural effect, I thought that Louis came with the full package to be —as he sold himself— enjoyed for a few days before saying farewell and then remembering him forever.

The dining room had gradually emptied of old glories and become full of new jubilant emotions. I felt different. Not better or worse, but simply different. It was as if my spirit had risen from the chair, leaving my skin and sad bones behind, to return as a toned spirit. It was a strange sensation to contemplate myself detached from all light, from all faith, from all; placed at the end of that tunnel of languid obscurities and withered truths. I felt more myself now. Even my nails had changed color when I returned from that astral journey. They were once again turquoise blue instead of the flesh color of carelessness and routines. Neither were they cut short to type better. They were the right length to gracefully scratch a grateful back. I felt different; rather, I felt from another time. Of a time that corresponded to me once but to which I gave way little by little over the years. I didn't want to think too much. The moment was mine... mine, and that of my basic instincts.

I decided to roll out the red carpet for Louis to that renewed self. "I'm having a pleasant time... with you."

Louis blushed, which was unexpected for a man who claimed to have enjoyed the company of dozens of women, even though he was still a virgin.

"I told you it would be fun." His answer was less romantic than expected.

"Tell me one thing. Why did you ask me in writing to have dinner?" I asked while tapping my new turquoise fingernails on the table and leaning toward him.

Louis shrugged and looked at the ceiling in a desperate search for the perfect answer.

"Actually, I... I didn't," he answered. "Do you want some more wine?" he added. "This special harvest always reminds me of—"

"What do you mean?" I interrupted. "You didn't ask me to dinner?"

Louis drank his wine very slowly, and, when he couldn't pretend to continue drinking, he confessed, "No. I simply brought you those pages, but, technically, I never asked you to dinner."

He was right! I rewound to the point of that conversation and found, to my dismay, that the damned one had never even suggested it. Actually, I invited myself, assuming that that was the reason for his visit. I felt so ridiculous... the rage began to bubble in my throat like lava.

"Anyway—" he said.

"Be quiet. Please be quiet," I interrupted with my eyes closed. "Don't say anything. Don't say anything and start kissing me before I change my mind!"

Louis, the man used to making women feel confused, was now confused. He looked around the room and realized that nothing was left but the intense desire to have sex. He jumped out of his chair and pounced on my lips. What began as a tame and sheepish kiss gradually turned into a wild and fierce display of passion. Without a second thought, he swept the table clear before placing me on it as the main course. I wrapped my legs around him and made him understand that I was no novice in the game of love. The ashtray and one of the glasses crashed onto the floor, but the shattering of glass did nothing but further inflame our passion. I grabbed him by his wavy mane and reined him in like a young foal.

But then, most inconveniently, the question of with whom he was planning to have dinner inexplicably crossed my mind. I murmured the question in his ear while his lips traveled along my neck.

"Don't worry about that now," he whispered.

"Who was she? Tell me..." I whispered again.

"It doesn't matter."

"Yes, it does matter," I insisted, raising my voice as I explored his earlobe.

"I like your perfume of peonies," he said as his lips grazed my neck.

I was impressed with his olfactory abilities, but that move didn't distract me from my original question: "With whom...?"

Louis, defeated, exhaled. Looking downcast, he pointed with his index finger and said, "With the woman sitting over there."

"With her!"

Out of sheer instinct, I wanted to shout, "With that bitch!" But I had no reason for saying so other than a catty attack of jealousy.

Louis apologized and then said, in the most child-like way, "I was wandering on the deck all morning with my letter in my hand and my invitation to dinner in my mouth, but you were dozing most of the time."

"And let me guess: you couldn't wait until the afternoon, and that's why you asked that other woman?"

Louis remained silent, with his face set in that irresistibly innocent look.

"But why did you change your mind?" I asked inquisitively.

"Because she doesn't blink," he answered immediately.

I couldn't help but explode into outrageous laughter.

"You're going to have to give me something better than that," I said, still wrapped in spasms of laughter.

"It's true... She doesn't blink. That woman does not blink and that baffles me," he said with the utmost sincerity, which made me laugh even more.

I suddenly stopped laughing and, giving him my most piercing look, said, "Give me something that puts my ego to rest, even if you must lie."

"Because you are far more erotic than her," he replied with no hesitation and with an irresistible manly look.

Louis knew exactly what kind of compliment to use according to the terrain: *intelligent* was the word of choice to cross the arid deserts, while *erotic* was of better use once he had arrived at the uncertain wetlands. As simple as that. And yet most men continue to mess it up at this truly cardinal point.

The whirlwind descended again, but this time the impetus gave way to a whole new waltz of skillful caresses, our breaths sending up gusts of steam like those of horses on a brisk autumn day. The quagmire of unrestrained feelings that is the attraction had by then reached every buttonhole of his shirt, every buckle of my shoes, every stitch of embroidery of my lingerie. We were at the point of no return when I suddenly had a terrifying thought: what if he decided to take me right there on the table? I feared neither because I didn't want it to happen nor because of the indiscretion of doing it in a public place, but because I unexpectedly remembered the words of my late grandmother, who always preached that nothing was sinful in life, as long as it is done where it should be. "Everything has its place," she used to say.

I pleaded in his ear, "Not here..."

But Louis had other plans. Like a magician, he violently yanked the tablecloth off the next table, bowing for me after his intrepid performance. That barbaric —almost primitive— gesture did not help to contain my libido.

"Let's go!" he said with the tablecloth in one hand, a bottle of wine in the other, and a foot on the service ladder that led to the upper deck, which was closed to the public.

"I can't do that…" I said, like a good girl.

"Same with me and the blinking!" he shouted, already on the upper deck.

Cocooned in laughter, like a madwoman, I scrambled up the rusty ladder and, looking down, realized that I was suspended in a chilling emptiness over the lake.

"Why can't we do it where everyone else—" I whispered.

"Because there are no stars there," said Louis, holding out his hand to help me up the last few rungs.

The night felt festive. Detached from reality, I felt almost like I was dancing with the stars. Cambodia was suspended in a cosmic broth where gravity had ceased to exist, immersed in a darkness so deep that even gray shades had perished, in a silence so solemn that it seemed like the funeral of music. And if something as basic as universal laws had vanished, why should we abide by any rules? I wondered.

Louis arranged the tablecloth of virginal white on the floor, improvising a bed of love that lacked only a few candles around it to be perfect. He did it with such devotion, with such care, with such tenderness, that more than desire, I felt an almost scientific curiosity to know how his hands would caress me if he was so considerate during the prelude. I knew I was destined to rejuvenate and shed thirty years. So it was.

While we lay on the tablecloth, he began to kiss my feet very softly, and did not stop until the tingling was so overwhelming that I gave way to childish giggling. He moved up my gelid calves, chilled from natural fear rather than the cold, but which soon began melting under his generous lips. He continued his journey, extinguishing the tremor in the flesh of my thighs with his warm kisses. He wandered freely and skillfully along my groin; more timidly, he then ambled through the central valleys, until a whine of pleasure escaped me.

He recognized the signal to remove the last layers of clothing from my body, and he did so with such gentleness and delight that I wondered whether it was an angel undressing me in the antechamber of heaven. But I suddenly remembered, horrified, a detail of my feminine condition that surely my uncontrolled subconscious had forgotten.

"Wait. I'm menstruating," I confessed, embarrassed.

"It doesn't matter," he said calmly.

And without giving the matter another thought, he continued his journey north of the equator of my waist, discovering that my belly was not carved from rock like the young steppes but instead had topography appropriate to my age. He dragged his cheek from the right flank of my abdomen to the opposite slope and then returned the same way with his other cheek.

"It's like a desert where you must search for the oasis," he said wisely.

He began drawing concentric circles, with my navel at the epicenter, and I knew he was rehearsing for the other forbidden well. He rejoiced in that well of glory in search of the nectar that had been left a little lower.

"This is the true center of the universe," he murmured.

I grabbed his curly hair and maneuvered him up to my chest to avoid further temptation. He responded by exploring the new orography with his fingertips. Using his forefinger and thumb, he cautiously inspected the tip of one of the hills, while with his lips he did the same on the neighboring peak. He entertained himself thus, jubilant and cheerful, for a few seconds that felt like a glorious wild fruit punch, while he presumably imagined having regressed to his sweet infancy. He placed his open hand over my chest and, with the help of my nipple, drew a hieroglyph on his palm.

"It was written..." said the oracle.

He then made the ascent to my shoulders and used his castaway's beard to please the skin across the entire length of my collarbone. An electric current ran from the base of my neck to my oregano field, which, during those days of carnal vigilance, was a hopeful patch of fresh mint rather than a dry bush. And maybe curious about what that same clandestine pecking could achieve on my neck, he began to kiss it, inch by inch, and the cartilage of my ear, to finally reach my defenseless nape.

Fearing my own predictable moaning, I grabbed his hand in despair and took his thumb into my mouth, turning it into a pacifier. I sucked it with such enthusiasm that my lover, probably confusing the finger with his own erect appendage, was the one who ended up howling like a jealous wolf howls at the moon. With adolescent impatience, Louis shimmied out of his underpants, mounted me, and sank firmly into me.

The first spasm came without warning. More than an orgasm, the sensual earthquake trailed aftershocks. It moved from a major to a minor key, like Strauss's *Also Sprach Zarathustra* followed by the nocturnes of Chopin. The second and third outbreaks of ecstasy were also rocky, though with a more contained feverishness, and from the fourth onward the outpouring of glory was almost a timid apology compared to the others.

Dawn found us naked and belly up. After an entire night of intense pleasure, I couldn't even open my eyes.

"We've done it like two youngsters, I said.

"That's what we are," Louis answered, half asleep.

When a righteous sun began to burn our rosy skins, the tinkling of the breakfast utensils downstairs was already impossible to ignore. After standing up, I observed Louis, who was still in the fetal position, lying on a tablecloth sown with the red roses of our bloodthirsty love.

When Louis noticed the spots, he said, amused, "I warned you I was a virgin."

# CHAPTER SEVEN

## PART FOUR: MEKONG

The ship moved relentlessly, finally reaching the river port nearest to Siem Reap. The lake waters had receded at that time of the year and, for fear of running aground on the sandbars, the captain ordered the anchor dropped off the coast. Our ship released two hoarse bellows that attracted a swarm of multicolored local barges, which promptly surrounded our *New Spring* to transport passengers to the harbor. The operation of transshipment of more than half a hundred passengers by that improvised wooden footbridge was announced as the highlight of the floating circus. And so, it was.

The maneuver became especially complex when it came to the crossing of one round, rosy-skinned woman, dressed as though she had stepped out of the past and carrying an aristocratic-looking pug puppy. The woman made several attempts to cross the footbridge, which rocked from side to side like a suspension bridge. Her frustration increased with the growing murmuring of the avid spectators and, especially, with the resounding shrieks of one of the most distinguished passengers' macaw, who with every attempt yelled at the top of its voice, "To hell if you cross!"

Its owner, a former French government official who spent half his life in French Guiana, later explained that he had acquired the animal from his former neighbors in the city of Cayenne. Apparently, the previous owners had spent the five years of their marriage arguing fiercely, always and about anything, but especially every time the husband was about to put a foot on the threshold to supposedly go play dominos after dinner at the club. The parrot had learned all sorts of curses, and it liked to shout them out, particularly in stressful situations.

The stout woman was still suffering from spasms due to the incessant screams of the damn parrot, and nothing and nobody could silence the bird. After a dozen unsuccessful attempts, the lady seemed to have come to terms with her own destiny, when, already halfway onto the catwalk, the macaw, copying what its former mistress told her husband's portrait once he died, screamed, "To hell you finally went!" The woman, panicking excessively, tightened her arms against her breasts, which propelled the dog out like a wet bar of soap.

The dog fell into the lake, and horror spread like wildfire through the ship, with some passengers empathizing with the dog, no doubt thinking about their own pets, and others with the woman, placing themselves in her shoes. Contemplating the absurdity of the situation, I felt fear of growing old. No villager jumped into the water to rescue the dog, and those who tried to use oars to rescue it were doing nothing more than smacking the poor animal. Before collective hysteria could set in, the captain finally took off his officer's uniform and, in a heroic act that earned him the purple cross, for the rest of the journey at least, dove into the water. He spent a few agonizing seconds threshing the bottom of the lake looking for the animal, which by then had presumably accepted its fatal destiny in the quagmire. But the captain eventually emerged, having accomplished his mission, proudly displaying the dog, which he had grabbed by one paw and was shaking like a hunted hare.

The applause was sensational, and the captain was filled with happiness at the ovation and the passenger's joy. The captain used a rope to climb out of the water, helping himself along with one hand and his sea-lion teeth while carrying under his arm the noble mutt, which was little more than a wad of mud but grateful not to be resting with the catfish in the lake. Once on deck and carried away by the moment, the captain raised his arms again in euphoric triumph and showed off the dog as a symbol of his unquestionable victory. His Homeric gesture only increased the hubbub, however. The captain was nude, and while showing off the rescued dog was also inadvertently showing off his hanging blunderbuss. In his haste to rescue the dog, he had stripped completely naked, forgetting that he now commanded a high-ranking vessel and no longer his own fishing barge.

"That thing deserves an extra trouser leg," the old woman next to me remarked lasciviously.

Louis and I, after almost forty-eight hours together and several rounds in bed, felt like a couple as close as any other.

"I knew you were destined for each other ever since I saw you two," said an old lady when she saw us getting off the boat holding hands.

Louis, with his characteristic smile, like that of a redeeming priest, responded by kissing her hand in a gentlemanly manner and saying, "Neither did I, I assure you, neither did I..."

A black *tuk-tuk* adorned with folkloric tablecloths awaited us as if we were disembarking from our honeymoon after having promised each other cotton clouds in church. The driver, a local with a fine bone structure and prominent clavicles, greeted us with a smile that showed more holes than teeth and, hurrying to fasten his ragged shirt, got ready to go. He apologized three times while refilling an improvised jerrycan, which was attached to the motorcycle to feed water into the cooling system. He started that metallic skeleton and took us stumbling over all the potholes he possibly could, making that Cambodian experience complete and memorable.

The heat was suffocating. But Louis didn't seem to mind that his white cotton shirt was stuck to his chest like a second skin, allowing a glimpse of his curly chest hair that looked as if it was born of the fabric of his shirt itself. He was happy in his fairy *tuk-tuk*, taking pictures of everyone and everything, greeting back everyone who greeted us, which was everyone. He photographed the unnamed treetops; the common rocks, which he said looked like pterodactyl bones; the rusty traffic signs; the houses sunk into the fabulous colored mud and those on high pillars over the fabled rice fields. He photographed the palm-roof houses of vagrants who had been upgraded to poor, and the zinc-roof houses of the poor, who were regarded as rich. He photographed the unused latrines and the disused wells, the birds that chirped invisibly, and the visible birds that didn't chirp. He photographed the old women with shaved hair that signified mourning and the young women with straight hair that signified life. He photographed the many skinny children who laughed at everything and the few fat ones who cried for nothing.

Louis' euphoria was such that, had I not known how well traveled he was, I would have thought that this was his first time out of the village. I wondered why I had lost part of that wonderful ability to surprise myself with the little things. Me, who used to press delicate flowers inside sturdy books; me, who used to collect fleeting thoughts and loose phrases with no apparent purpose; me, who failed algebra and was incapable of formulating equations with letters without adding some wider metaphor to them; me, who transformed you little by little, conscientiously, while I transformed myself, unconsciously. I even became angry with myself when I realized that had I carried sweets in my purse, I wouldn't have thrown them to the children, thinking some stupid World Bank policy prevented me from such a spontaneous act. I'm sure I first would've assessed the sustainability of the intervention or the potential side effects to the beneficiaries. All good practices, of course, in the context of multimillion-dollar aid to poor countries, but of no help in daily acts of kindness. It was frightening to see how much our professional ethos affects our personal habits. And, while I racked my brain as these circular thoughts ran through my mind, I saw Louis take out some mint chocolates, which he had presumably stolen in handfuls from the ship's bar and throw them with complete impunity to the children who ran after the *tuk-tuk*.

"Children love chocolate," he said innocently.

The *tuk-tuk* driver joyfully explained that before taking us to the temples of Angkor, he first had to pass by the health center for his morning infusion. We didn't understand what the hell he was talking about until we saw him exiting the health facility with a drip hanging from a bamboo pole and a cannula inserted into his wrist. The driver attached the bamboo to a purpose-built metal bracket on the *tuk-tuk* and then lit a cigarette that was little more than a filter. Grinning toothlessly, he said, "A drink and a cigar, just like Westerners do at weddings."

Louis and I for a moment forgot, or wanted to forget, that this was not our honeymoon, but rather a trick of destiny, a divine design or something like that. Although we knew it was all a mirage, we chose the adventure of living above the leaden feeling of having lived already. Intoxicated by a happiness as transient as it was deceptive, my fingers interlaced with his in a clumsy maneuver after I pretended to startle at one of the bumps in the road. Louis corresponded, similarly pretending that it was a natural move, but he made it even worse when he started talking about random things. I believe it was helicopters.

"They are very noisy, that's the problem," he said.

I had to turn away so that Louis wouldn't notice me closing my eyes while I reveled in the feeling of the whiplash of love. Falling in love is worth everything, I thought to myself. It was a cottony sensation that left on the palate the sweet taste of the milk cakes couples in love eat alongside the Rambla of Montevideo. When remembering the capital of Uruguay, the memories of the two of us —you and I— strolling together through its cobbled streets came to mind inconveniently, as well as a momentary rage, I think brought on by feeling, unjustifiably, that I was being unfaithful to you. But I quickly crossed the abyss, and before Louis could come up with other nonsense, I gave him a kiss as that left him floating on air during the time I needed to shake off the ghosts of the past. The *tuk-tuk* driver looked at us intermittently in the rear mirror, delighted by the tender game that was taking place back there.

"You have your television, and I have mine," he declared with astonishing sincerity.

Angkor Wat revealed itself with a nakedness only threatened by the virgin forest looming around its walls. Its five sandstone barbicans rose up like the towers born when you let the wet sand slide through your fingers on the beach. The reflection of the huge stone city on the lagoon invited us to travel back to a mystical time in which strapping warriors wore fabulous rhinestones and were mounted on steeds with muscled chests and manes braided with precious metals; to that bygone time when the sunsets were lyrical and life felt different. The scattered palm trees created the feeling of a blurred watercolor in the impressionist style, while skinny men competed for palmtops pregnant with voluptuous coconuts, dashing dates, and generous fruits laden with honey. In the distance, monks dressed in exultant orange walked in line, adding a punch of color amid so much green. The long stone bridge that connected the everyday world with the historical city invited us to walk through. We did so like two hypnotized souls, like two enchanted wanderers, like two fools in love.

Louis let out a deep sigh and said, "Just like sex: the more I come, the more I want to come."

At the entrance to the temple, a group of maimed, crippled, and blind musicians, all of them disfigured by antipersonnel mines, played their *trunks* with violin bows around a huge *roneat* that sounded like a sad xylophone.

They sounded like a ruined band lamenting human dispossession, but the moment oozed humanity with every note. They sold their improvised music in exchange for the few *riels* tourists had the will to donate. Louis and I sat on a rug tacked with multicolored straw and let ourselves be swallowed by those out-of-tune sounds that talked about a dissonant life too. The musicians, whom most tourists ignored, felt flattered by our presence and recomposed themselves. The deaf musician hit the blind musician with his bow, signaling that it was time to return to the world of the living to give everything for a few minutes. The music gained in volume what it lost in harmony. Nevertheless, we thanked them for their efforts with profuse applause and occasional standing ovations that confused the passing tourists, some of whom even stopped to make sure that it was really us, and not them, who had a distorted notion of art.

"This can't be seen everywhere!" shouted Louis to passing Germans.

"Fortunately!" they replied.

And just when our eardrums had come to terms with those stray harmonics, one of the musicians, who wore a patch over his left eye and who was missing his right ear, decided to delight us with his angelic voice. It was remarkable. Had that sound come out of a cat it would have seemed inexplicable but coming from a human body it was simply mystical. For some reason, I felt uncomfortable, and, just when I made a move to stand up, Louis took me by the wrist, suggesting that I should stay there for a little longer.

"The merit is not in the music but in the story behind," he said.

Later, we walked for hours until we reached the less frequented areas, dotted with minor temples and ruins devoured by the vegetation. Some inhabited villages had become overgrown by the jungle too. Guided by the locals and our own imagination, we finally found the community where Louis intended to interview a local activist. She had become famous for opposing the concessions the government granted to logging companies, which indiscriminately cut down the forests, thus destroying the livelihood of hundreds of communities. Despite the many attempts made by the police to keep her in jail, they had never been able to imprison her for more than a few days. She was always released, inexplicably, and with no charges, which was paradoxical in a country where one could spend months in jail for no reason. Her name was Boupha, which in Khmer means "like a flower."

We were received with unusual suspicion. Soon we understood that the villagers were accustomed to visits from the authorities —or from men in black, as they described them— all to intimidate Boupha and convince her to abandon her personal crusade. Louis tried to calm them down by explaining that we were there to talk about their cause. He managed to earn their trust, but all the time we waited for Boupha to return from her campaign of the day, we were kept under strict surveillance, and the villagers never let go of their machetes.

After more than an hour of sitting on a log and drinking coconut water, a group of motorcycles appeared in the village, all showing the banners they had apparently used that day to protest against Boupha's imprisonment of the month. The motorcyclists made an entrance, raising dust and blowing their horns in the spirit of celebration.

They began to roll in a circle, leaving in their center a woman who we assumed was Boupha. The dust lent a mystical air to the woman, who seemed extolled to the status of goddess. The guard who had sat by our side told us happily, "They never get to keep her in jail for more than a day or two."

After a few minutes of tribal celebration, the motorcycles dispersed, revealing behind a curtain of smoke the subject of our investigation: Boupha. She was a woman in her sixties, immortal in appearance, with long ash-colored hair. Her inner strength bestowed upon her an intimidating depth, and she walked with an intensity born of incandescent momentum. She extended her arm decisively and greeted us with a handshake that felt very Western.

"Are you the writer from the international tribunal?" she asked. "I was expecting you," she added, without giving Louis a chance to respond.

We followed her up to a large barrel that, sliced in two, served as a bathtub. She began to clean herself, freely and without shame and without losing the thread of her monologue. She told us how the government was selling the country to the highest bidder, without any distinction based on the ultimate intentions of each buyer, to new and old enemies, regardless of their political tendency or religion.

"The one that brings the largest envelope gets the land," she said calmly but bitterly. "You will have already seen that from Phnom Penh to Siem Reap there are only rice fields and the occasional sad coconut tree. But no forest that exceeds the size of a small garden. They are cutting everything down, little by little, and the worst thing is that they throw their people off the land, sentencing them to death, if not of hunger, of sadness for sure. There is nothing left of the legendary Cambodia. Nothing. The other day a tourist asked me if there were tigers around here. Tigers! Imagine! The last time I saw a tiger was when I was little and the circus came to town... Tigers? If you want to see tigers, go to the capital and ask for any ministry, I told him."

Louis wasn't sure when to take the floor in front of that tigress in the skin of a woman.

"But you have not come all this way to hear stories about tigers, right?" Boupha asked.

"No," Louis answered, smiling. "Actually, I came to talk about love."

Boupha's gaze turned leaden and, after a long silence, she said, "That other tiger. I have seen him even less."

After an exhalation that could encompass the entire universe, she began to narrate: "I used to call him Chea, although that's not his real name."

Chea was nineteen years old when they both met at the Faculty of Law at the University of Phnom Penh. I had assumed that Boupha came from a humble background, but apparently, she came from an academic lineage, like Chea, and her father was once the rector of the university. Boupha and Chea became friends over a conversation at the campus cafeteria, where, over coffees and croissants, they started dreaming of changing the world. That was in the context of the first student revolts, protesting social inequality in a country that was reborn after independence. They also bonded thanks to the university newspaper, where both were editors, and where they often found themselves exchanging intoxicating poems of impossible love. Inspired by one of those verses, he once told her, "One day we will go around the world together," and she replied, already a visionary, "Why only once?"

They came together one sunset when she, leaning against an acacia brimming with yellow flowers, listened to his whispers filled with half-truths that she chose to believe in full. They bonded over her confession of wanting to share a life with him, day after day, until death parted them. He answered, "Me too," but added that he planned to die young, and she replied that that didn't matter because she would still love him in the afterlife. In the times of peace, all that and much more united them. War split them apart.

When Khmer Rouge soldiers stormed the university campus, they both knew that their adventure among books, poems, and glories had come to an end. The soldiers went for the intellectuals, for those who knew how to write, for those who knew more than they did; even the ones who simply wore glasses were deemed counterrevolutionaries. If on the top of that they found you at the university, the chances of disguising yourself as a villain were zero.

They were handcuffed and hoisted up by a group of soldiers, one of whom snapped, "To keep you is no gain; to kill you is no loss." But instead of filling them with lead right there, the soldiers decided to send them off to a re-education camp. There they were classified as *new people* and forced to work in the construction of infinite irrigation channels. *New people* was the term used by the Khmer Rouge to refer to the urban population, while *old people* were all those from the rural areas, who mostly worked in agricultural activities. The *old people* were chosen by the

Khmer Rouge to repopulate Cambodia after the purges. The *new people* simply had to disappear —that was the motto of the *Angka*, the supreme power of the Khmer Rouge.

They put a rifle in Chea's hands and made him believe that those Cambodians who came from the city were the enemy and should be watched while digging irrigation canals from sunrise to sunset. Enemies! Enemies made of lean bodies, fed on coconut water, palm honey, and watery rice... Dara was one of those boys from the city who Chea had to watch while they were rotting in the swamps, where the water lilies had thrived before. Dara was a year younger than Chea. Only six months earlier he wore a plaid shirt, combed his hair with a parting to the side, and sat in the classrooms of the Polytechnic School where he learned radio electronics. Now he was an enemy of the state, paradoxically, for studying the very same subject that Pol Pot himself —the supreme leader of the Khmer Rouge— had studied, only in Cambodia, instead of in Paris, as Pol Pot did. Dara happened to also be a cousin of Boupha, and the three of them together had founded the student newspaper while at University.

After six months in the concentration camp, Boupha digging nonstop and Chea watching the prisoners, as ordered to by the leader, the guards wanted to test Chea's loyalty. Thus, the camp leader approached him from behind, put a gun in his hands, and, referring to Dara, said, "He tried to escape last night. Kill him."

Dara shared his barracks with Chea. He had spent the previous night awake in the cabin, trying to fix a transistor with the aim of hearing news from Phnom Penh, where he had lost track of his two little sisters.

"Are you hesitating?" the voice insisted from behind.

Dara, only three meters from Chea, knew he was dead while alive. He pretended not to have heard anything and kept digging. His tears fell to the mud while he thought of all the beautiful moments he had lived with his family. Boupha, just a few meters away from both, knew that Chea only had two options, and that only in one their mutual love would survive the shot. Chea also knew that spilling Dara's innocent blood would cause a hemorrhage in his relationship with Boupha. But finally, he chose what every living being ultimately wants: to continue living.

That same night, alive on the outside yet dead inside, Boupha approached the barracks where Chea was. She found him in a complete state of desolation and, in a futile attempt to comfort him as he cried, she told him, "It was his life or yours."

But she said it with no conviction. And, after drying his tears as best she could, Chea looked her in the eye and asked in a way that allowed no lies, "Tell me, would you have saved yourself?"

Boupha lowered her head and didn't answer. He immediately knew then that the revolutionary vision that had brought them together, the canvas on which the future was painted, had suddenly cracked.

Months passed by, and each day became a struggle to survive. But the worst part to bear was the icy wall that grew between them. They knew they were victims of a macabre destiny over which they had no control, and yet they were unable to close the wound that the gunpowder had left on their souls. They could do nothing but contemplate each other from a distance, like observing each other from within the depths of a canyon, as if waiting for life itself to shoot what remained of their wounded love. But because neither of them had the courage to put an end to their dreams, it was finally him who, resorting to charm, managed to persuade the camp leader to move him to another camp, where he could better serve the spirit of that meaningless revolution.

"He always had the ability to convince the very devil that life was better in heaven," explained Boupha.

The morning that Chea was preparing himself to leave, Boupha decided to break the silence. She approached the truck onto which Chea was climbing, and said, "I'll continue here, truthful to myself, planting trees to make this place less gray."

To which he replied, "And I promise to be your invisible guardian angel in your crusade."

After listening to this story, the three of us remained immersed in a strange solitude we each dealt with in our own way. Boupha, perhaps, imagined herself there amid those cursed rice fields, desiring to change the past. Louis, I presume, revived his own ghosts, whose existence I had started to envisage, although its true nature was still a mystery to me. Meanwhile, I fought my own ghosts.

As the silence became as prolonged as it was uncomfortable, I decided to break it with a statement that turned out to be most inopportune. "At least you're fulfilling your part of the deal," I said.

Staring into my eyes, Boupha replied with a mix of kindness and defiance, "And so did he, my darling, and so did he…"

As she said those words, she put her hand into her bra to retrieve something that turned out to be an old photograph, safely encased in plastic. She began to caress it, and then she kissed it before bringing it closer to her chest to cradle it. I stretched my neck trying to see what looked like an aged photo of Chea and her in the old days at the university. Surprised, I exclaimed, "But that man is—!"

Boupha's gaze turned feline again and, with the agile movements of a jealous panther, she put the photo back into her bra. Louis, who was quick to guess that I had inconveniently identified some familiar face in the country, told Boupha, apologetically, "She works for the World Bank."

Boupha's appearance lost its initial state of grace. Disconcerted, she began to murmur nonsense, complaining about all the things she had to do before the next day. "It's getting late," she repeated several times. "I shouldn't have taken it out," she muttered.

The bitter taste left by history intensified because of the uncomfortable situation I had caused. I cursed myself for not having been more discreet. Louis and I knew we were not welcome there anymore. Louis, somewhat annoyed, and, I, disgusted by my own observation, said our final words, which sounded like a prayer, and began our retreat.

Just before I left, Boupha took me by the arm and said with the voice of a young woman, "Wait. If you see him again, tell him that the reason I would never have pulled the trigger was to keep our love alive, even if dead myself."

We decided to slowly walk back. The afternoon had become lukewarm. Something inside us as well. The sunlight penetrated the forest, splitting into fine beams, which generated a mystical, almost ghostly, sensation. The carpet of leaves felt crunchy and deep as I stepped over it, while the trapped humidity my footsteps released brought back the memory of the flowery walls. The tender mosses fought to conquer the bark of the trees, not caring much whether they spread north or south, while the insects climbed inexorably up the trunks, trying to reach the sun, up, up, in search for life, where the birds waited, bringing them death.

Suddenly, in the middle of that fabulous silence, Louis paused and said, "So much orderly mess!"

He could have said something like, "It's getting a little late, maybe we should go back," or, "What time is your flight next week?" But no. He said what he said, and although it didn't make much sense, at the same time it made complete sense to me. Those are the kinds of magical expressions one only says at the beginning of a relationship.

Again, an old obsession: love. We are surrounded by it. Are we not? Most songs sing about love, most books are written about love, most films are mere images tinted with love. And yet we know almost nothing about it. We research the stars, which are so far away and don't even illuminate the world, but we spend so little time trying to better understand the things nearby, like love, which save us from the shadows. We research the meaning of the minuscule and rare things instead of trying to better understand the greatness and constant effect of love. We research how to extend life beyond reason, when lack of love is surely the most likely cause of death.

By the time we reached the walls of Angkor Thom, the twilight was already being announced by the white spectral birds migrating south, by the giant loud croaking frogs, by the golden flashes over the coppery waters. We climbed on top of its wide wall and walked along it, heading southwest, in search of the magical hour, just as the insects did, but hoping to find more life at the end. It was the golden hour: that short time window when light changes from white to orange, tinting everything in pure magic. From up there, the temples of Angkor could be seen, majestic and timeless, one of the wonders of the world. There was no doubt as to why those warriors of the past had built those fortresses where they did. It felt like we were at the center of the universe.

Amid the idyllic sunset, and with the sun already divided in two by the horizon, I felt Louis's full vigor at my back, with his forge-like heat, his jaguar prowl, and his manly body. I found it hard to breathe, maybe because he inhaled all the air, or perhaps it was his sheer presence. Whatever the reason, my breath became a stony sigh, a tormented gasp, and my skin began to ooze essential oils that soaked my white linen dress until it became transparent. By the time Louis dove his nose into my hair, inhaling deep like a ferocious wolf, I had already devoured my lower lip trying not to release the girly moan that I finally freed.

When he finally got out of my hair, he said, "You carry half a forest in here."

Using the excuse that the walk had been long and my legs were fatigued, I leaned back against him while he rested against a rock. And that's when he did something intrepid. Only his incorrigible charm saved him from being exposed by my defenses as a virtuous woman. He introduced his warm hands under my Hellenic dress and gradually started to climb with his fingertips up my thighs, following the trail of dripping molasses, presumably caused by the heat. And when he reached the top of my thighs,

Louis continued his search for the holy grail of love. There it was, an oasis that he perhaps thought he would find dry, but quite the opposite: it was lush and ready.

"Yes..., still young," I said.

Suddenly I could breathe freely while he panted like a greyhound after a hunt. The furtive explorer, overwhelmed by the treasure he found, began to retreat to safer regions. But I stopped his hands.

"Stay there. These sunsets don't happen twice."

He smiled like a fox and returned to his unaccomplished mission, less exploratory, more decisive this time. He resumed his journey through the tulip, putting aside the adorning sepals, until he reached the very chalice of the flower. He played freely, almost experimental, releasing jubilant music through every pore of my skin. The birds fluttered wildly above our heads in a similar state of grace and celebration, while those ethereal butterflies that were his hands in action fluttered underneath my skirt, which had become like a ghost in a castle.

"I will never understand how all the complexity of the woman up there becomes so simple down here," Louis said.

Thus, the conqueror, stimulated by the new orography, became curious and groped about those folds, despised before as mere doors to the anteroom, and which, while indeed serving as a prelude to something better, were also worthy of attention themselves. He rode by those dunes and slid randomly north to south, south to north, all along the valley between. Noticing that my body responded gratefully, he decided to go deeper and more closely explore the miracle of life. He came down the legendary

Mound of Venus, ready to make history. However, right at the edge of the cliff he hesitated once more.

"You're blessed," I whispered in his ear.

There was no need to insist anymore. Feeling like the chosen one, he started shedding glory right and left. Almost biblically, some purple clouds began to form on the horizon, which with perfect timing discharged beautiful rain that coincided with other minor storms that resounded throughout my body. After a couple more thunderstorms, which included lightning and sparks, we ended up lying on the grass, faint from love —or whatever it was that we did— me, contemplating those ruins and asking myself if we had perhaps profaned a sacred temple; Louis, innocently removing, one by one, the petals of another flower he had grabbed.

I whispered, "In nature everything feels natural."

# CHAPTER EIGHT

## PART FIVE: MEKONG

A faint indigo light penetrated through the fish-eye window of Louis's cabin. Dust motes floated fluorescently, as if our room were a fantastic galaxy and we the wake left by that same fantasy. His last words just before falling asleep had been, "I don't like perfect women; I don't find them enigmatic." As he breathed, asleep, like a peaceful bear, I wavered up and down with his rhythm, reflecting over the meaning of that phrase. A terrifying parallelism between you and him almost made me jump out of bed, alarmed and still naked. How had I not realized before! An acute fear, vertigo even, spread through me. To that day, I had held you in some kind of glass-spun urn, safe from everything and everyone. But that armored glass was now becoming thinner and thinner, like the crystallized sugar on the apple. The more I knew Louis, the more enigmatic I found him, and curiosity was always my weakness.

On the deck, while I was having breakfast alone, I tried to distract myself with my favorite pastime: creating lives for those around me. Thus, the waiter in his immaculate white uniform, the one that scurried across the deck carrying tea left and right, was the youngest of five brothers in a humble family. He always wanted to be, like his older brother, a snake charmer, not because he was attracted to those cold and slippery reptiles, but because he thought that the art of hypnosis would be a transferable skill to achieve an ultimate goal: to enchant the love of his life. She was a seller of palm liquor at the street market, a mysterious young lady with luminescent green eyes whose voice seduced any buyer passing by. Since he was twelve, he had been in love —in silence— with that incredible girl. Unfortunately, she was of Vietnamese origin, which was cause for suspicion on the part of both families, although her father had made it clear that ethnic differences were outdated and that with adequate financial compensation the matter would certainly be resolved. For this reason, the boy ran around the boat trying to capture every tip that could bring him closer to her lips.

The young waiter, while quietly immersed in his fairytale, served tea to a woman who had presumably just turned forty. I watched the latter with amazement as she almost ruthlessly attacked a huge basket filled with green apples. The woman, who wore a necklace of magnificent pearls wrapped around her neck in three unequal lengths, was taking the apples one by one and devouring them with great enthusiasm —I would almost say with anger— without even sparing their hearts. It didn't appear normal. On the occasions that I had witnessed someone attacking food this way it had either been due to prolonged famine —which could be ruled out in this case— or because of a broken heart.

Suddenly I noticed an important detail. On the table was also a small pile of what looked like a shredded letter. The diagnosis was clear: lovesickness. I imagined then that he, the correspondent, was a Balinese painter of still life fruit images, while, she, with her unrequited love, was a regional marketing assistant of the United Fruit Company. They had met recently, when he was hired to design the sketches for a new advertising campaign and she was visiting Bali to evaluate the proposal. He wanted to show her his enchanted studio, located on the summit of a volcano known by the locals as the Mountain of Fog. She was immediately carried away by those stormy summits, and unconsciously erased from her mind the other storms she had left behind in Maryland, where she lived. For some inexplicable reason, she found observing him while he painted all those enormous green apples on large canvases irresistible. Perhaps because of the solvent vapors, maybe because of the reduced concentration of oxygen at those heights, she felt volatile and disembodied. Poetry followed painting, and confessions followed next; confessions that sounded like verses poisoned with doubts.

Lost in a labyrinth of emotions, there was no other escape but to declare, "Have you ever felt so imprisoned that you wanted to scream loud, very loud?"

To which he responded without hesitation, "What do you think I built this studio up here for?"

And then the two began to scream like mad, first filled with tears of laughter and later with tears of sadness. And as blues and love share similar notes, to the sounds that started as a timid sobbing, others of a more celebratory nature followed, which eventually culminated in a Homeric song worthy of a climax of conquest. They made healthy love without contemplations. And only on the last night of the three days the romance lasted, they confessed, now amid uncontrolled crying, that their hearts were committed to other people.

While she was packing, he had left a note in a small pocket, a note she would only notice weeks later, when she thought she had already gotten over those three magical days. The message read, in capital letters, "A GREEN APPLE WILL ALWAYS REMEMBER ME OF THE BITTERNESS OF YOUR TROUBLED HEART." That was the note she had torn apart on the table.

Just as she was about to attack another of those innocent apples, a gust of air made all the pieces of the note fly across the deck. At that precise moment, a man with an immaculate beard, who walked with the aid of an ivory-handled cane, caught several of the papers on the fly and looked at them with enthusiasm, as if they were messages that had arrived from heaven. He then moved meekly to where the woman was and sat down next to her, as if coming to announce some prophecy. "Love and chance are fruits of the same tree, you know?" he said calmly. Then he arranged the pieces of paper on the table and began to play to form a sentence with the written words.

"Look here: 'YOUR HEART WILL ALWAYS REMEMBER ME GREEN.' Now I understand everything, Miss: you are a princess, and he was a prince turned into a toad." The woman wiped her damp eyes and could not help erupting in a stormy laugh that cleared a little the black clouds that had hovered over her. And with that presumably sincere move, the man invited himself to her table, and, later, into her life as well. First, he kept playing with the ripped-up note, trying to construct a longer phrase. Yet he couldn't. And as the man was lame in one foot but skilled at word games, he confessed with as much serenity as confidence, "I wanted to impress you with a phrase that spoke of how beautiful you are, but I'm afraid these words are insufficient. I apologize." He made a move to get up, and, she, moved by his sincerity, invited him to stay and have coffee.

I continued to imagine that perhaps driven by the momentary emptiness left by her Balinese love, or maybe daunted by the chronic solitude of her marriage, she decided to check the veracity of the saying that love has no age. She asked the old man to accompany her to the piano bar on the deck, where she most innocently enticed him to talk about life and its miracles. Later, at twilight, they naturally floated up to the restaurant, where they dined on river lobster and aphrodisiac oysters from imaginary seas. She became carried away by the conversation and her fantasies of being a mermaid, and, between smiles and toasts to life, she ended up confessing that she always wanted to be a magician and not what she actually was. He, who was not an old pervert, but who wasn't made of stone either, began to imagine her dressed up as an illusionist, in those tight costumes in which not even the smallest bunny could fit. With the pretext of going to the bathroom, he took his blue pill of love, because he anticipated he would need a real trick to live up to the illusion.

As expected, their boat drifted until it ran aground exactly where they envisioned it would from the second bottle of wine: in heaven. Already in bed, she continued talking to him about her existential doubts, about how life was complex and feelings even more so, as if asking her father for life advice. She finally discovered that his words were wise and his intentions noble, but his vigor withered at dawn, and so did his breath.

Back to reality, we arrived at the next village, the weather had conspired to make it look like a sunset. Purple clouds threatened a storm, something unusual for that time of year. There was no breeze, no sound, no sensation of cold or heat, as in the false calm that precedes the tempest. We were setting off for one of the last interviews Louis had planned on his trip. The next morning, our ship would sail downriver to its starting point: Phnom Penh. I had noticed his gradual silence since the night before, though I didn't know whether to attribute it to our sleep deprivation or to the fact that there was only one more day left on board that dreamy cruise.

Once in the tuk-tuk on the way to the village where we had to do the interview, all our conversation consisted of short phrases and simple references to what we were observing along the way. When we arrived and while descending from the tuk-tuk, Louis half confessed to himself, "I'm not sure what I'm going to find here." It was a lost village, one of those that probably did not even show up on the map. A bunch of tilted palm trees had made room for the few wooden houses adorned with palm roofs. Chickens and a few free-range ducks roamed around, going back and forth to a half-evaporated pond, where the quagmire served as refreshment in those torrid months. The rice fields, by then dry, remembered that everything is cyclical; and thank goodness that it is, because in this way one has the certainty that bad things eventually pass, although good things unfortunately too. This was a place where not the hands of the clock, but the time of life and death dictated its timeless routine.

Guided by the directions of the locals, Louis managed to find the house indicated in his notes. It was a house like any other: wooden, palm, poor. As we approached, a shadow crept from within, which later became an old woman of well past seventy, with a rough face and a prominent skeleton. Louis explained why we were there, although the old woman showed no sign of interest. She seemed to live behind a cardboard mask. Louis asked if he could talk to any of her daughters, and she pointed to the two women who were washing their clothes in a basin. Louis watched them for a moment and then asked, "Do you have any more children?"

The old woman was going to answer, when a yellow dog began to chase the chickens and a stir of feathers added some action to that picture moored in time. Louis responded with a strange gesture that I didn't know whether to interpret as sadness or rancor. Louis held the woman's gaze for a few seconds and then said, "Let's go. It was a mistake coming here."

However, as we were making our way back to the *tuk-tuk*, Louis suddenly tensed. He had noticed the presence of another old woman sitting at the side of the house with her back against the wall, swaying back and forth while muttering unintelligible prayers. The old woman had a grayish gaze, eyes veiled in cataracts, and deformed arthritic fingers. Louis stopped and hesitated for a moment before moving toward her with short steps, as if he had discovered a living treasure. She was. He squatted in front of her and remained silent before almost boldly plucking a pink flower from a nearby bush and placing it in her hair. I thought it was a grotesque situation. She looked like an old madwoman disguised as a schoolgirl, although I imagine he was looking at her with different eyes.

"Are you Champei?" Louis asked.

The old woman raised her head slightly and, barely breaking her rhythm, fixed her gaze on the infinite and continued with her monologue.

"Don't stress: she's not deaf, but she can't hear either. My aunt lives in her own world," intervened one of the women. "Many remained like this after the war."

"Your aunt's name is Champei?" Louis asked.

"Yes," she answered.

Louis's eyes lit up. "Do you have a sister named Thida?" he stuttered excitedly.

The woman remained silent, but then replied, "Are you from the court for war crimes?"

"No. But one of the judges is a good friend of mine," answered Louis.

"They came here one day. We already told them everything we know. I was very small when my sister left home. I almost don't remember it. We also told them that Thida never came back from Phnom Penh."

Louis dropped his eyes to the ground. He remained motionless. Before he could react, the woman added, "Wait here; there's a letter from Thida that my aunt Champei brought back from the city."

The woman entered the house and soon returned with an envelope that had turned to sepia from which she took three sheets of paper covered in handwriting front and back, with the ink running in places. Louis took the letter as if life was corresponding with him from the past and then sat down on the decayed remains of a cart. Absorbed, he began to read it.

*Phnom Penh, April 19, 1975*
*Beloved mother:*

*It's been almost three years since you sent me to Phnom Penh to help Aunt Champei in the kitchen of the house where she worked. Neither when I lived in the village nor in these last years in the city have I received your affection. I do not blame you: love is sometimes a luxury for the poor.*

*I was only sixteen when you put me into a cart pulled by oxen and sent me alone to the unknown. I cried all the way, which lasted almost five days, and I kept crying at night until I ran out of tears and dried up inside. I felt fear, a deep and dark fear. Everything in the city was strange to me: the noise of cars, the speed of the people, the clothes of its inhabitants, even the Khmer they spoke was different. I felt so alone. I missed my little sisters and the simple games that we spent each afternoon playing in the lagoon near home. Life in the village was simple, perhaps with no future, but it was my life, and even in times of hunger I was happy there, happy to have you close and, above all, to have my sisters, whom I feared I would never see again when you sent me away.*

*The first days in my new home were confusing, but Aunt Champei was good to me. She put me in her room and let me sleep beside her, so I would not feel afraid. She always took care of me like a mother. We live in a beautiful house, in the servants' annex of the French consul, although this is something that I understood only months after my arrival. At first, I did not even know what the word "consul" meant. I was a girl from the village, who only knew that this was a dream palace, like the dollhouse I once saw in a magazine that the wind blew into the village. It is a huge two-story mansion with high ceilings and walls painted bright yellow like a lemon, and a beautiful garden where frangipanis grow everywhere, spreading their sweet fragrance on warm April nights. In this dollhouse, I have spent three years helping Aunt Champei in the kitchen. Later I helped with other household chores too. The surprising thing is that what first felt like a prison finally ended up becoming the home of my life.*

*A short life, yes, but there are lives that are lived in only a moment. Mine is perhaps one of them.*

*I want you to know that I write this letter out of love. Yes, I have known love. Mother, I know that he is a boy who will one day become the man that every woman hopes to have. The man capable of loving a woman until he makes her feel that life is all about love, and everything else is just the background for love. The man who is difficult to have in times of peace and impossible to find in times of war. He is the man that you, mother, would not even think could exist, because there are none in the village. And that is why I no longer blame you for anything, mother, because I have felt something so precious and now I feel sorrow for those who live without love.*

*When I arrived here, the boy, the only son of the consul, was fifteen years old. I was sixteen and had no family. I almost didn't notice him until months after I arrived. He spent most of his time in his room, reading books and writing things that I could not read, because I did not know how. Sometimes I would see him in the garden, reading with his father or chatting with him while he smoked his pipe. He looked like an adult when he talked to his father, but I sensed that behind his quiet facade there was a whole world to be discovered. He was proper with the staff, as was his whole family, but I never saw him speaking with anyone other than his father, with whom he had a special relationship, and, at times, with his mother. I did not see him with friends, although he must have had some at the French Lyceum, where he studied. He is a handsome boy, with curly hair, wise hands, and a calm look. One of those people who quickly make you feel as if you have always known them and who show so much confidence that you want to confess everything, even your most intimate secrets. I think it is because of his eyes, I do not know, but you begin to talk and talk, and by the time you realize, you have already told him everything about you. And the best thing is that you feel happy to have told.*

*The first time I caressed his lips, he was bedridden after several weeks of convalescing with typhoid fever. He was so weak that I thought he was going to die. Someone in the village who looked like that would not have lasted two days. I brought food to him in bed, and he barely opened his eyes to eat. Some days I even had to help him by giving him the celery soup that the doctor ordered. Afterward, I would clean his lips with the tip of a napkin and arrange the pillows so that he could rest more comfortably. One day when I cleaned his lips, I noticed a blister from the fever. I decided to prepare an ointment made of coconut butter, mixed with oil and minced mint, and began to apply it to his lips at the end of each meal using my own fingers. He responded with a faint voice, grateful, and then slept soundly until the next meal.*

*The days went by, and I continued with my routine of feeding and caring for him. But one morning his mother suddenly opened the door and found me treating his lips. She did not seem to like it. She politely asked me to leave the room. The next day when I went to bring food to him, another maid told me that she had been asked to take care of the boy. I was sad because being by his side was the best part of my day. He finally recovered from his illness. I was glad to see him continue with his quiet and mysterious ways. I thought he would not remember my caring for him. But I was wrong.*

*One night when I went to bed, I found a poem written in French under my pillow. I could not sleep at night, dazed with a new strange feeling born out of nowhere. With the first sun, I rose to enter the dining room, where I quietly used a dictionary to discover what the verses said. I managed to find only the words of the title: lotus flower. And since I had no way of communicating with him, I decided to decorate the table where they ate with a large glass vase, in which I placed four lotus flowers as if floating in a pool. Then, to make sure he understood my message, I began to decorate every corner of the house with lotus flowers of all colors. The house was now full of floating flowers, and his father called me Rumchong Strei (the lotus girl) when I served the food at the table. He and his father smiled tenderly; his mother did not.*

*I felt so happy person knowing that I was no longer invisible. That same afternoon, while I was in my room, he knocked on my door, asked permission to enter, as if apologizing, and sat next to me on the bed. He brought with him the same poem translated into Khmer. He began to read it as best he could. I understood nothing — and yet all at the same time. That was the start of our secret language sessions.*

*The weeks went by, and our encounters became more and more frequent. We looked for each other throughout the house at all times. Time did not pass fast enough when we were apart. We never met outside the house, and yet our love was so immense that our small world was sufficient. We spent rainy afternoons hidden in the attic, he reading his history books, and me reading notebooks in French for beginners with drawings in the margins. We barely exchanged words. The mere company of human warmth was enough. Sometimes, a soft caress when turning the page was enough to add magic.*

*A first inexperienced and fleeting kiss on his birthday was followed by others lasting until dawn. On days when his parents were on official trips, we woke with our lips still glued together after having exchanged our breath for an eternal night. From that first nervous moment when our fingers intertwined with awkwardness, other times came when we caressed each other's hands, as if reading in them the future we did not have. The virginity that I thought I would lose in the swampy rice fields, I gave to him surrounded by the lotus flowers in his room.*

*We invented a new world in the long afternoons that we spent hiding in the attic. We called it Calandria. It lived in our imagination; and our imagination lived in it. In this world we invented fantasy, to keep the magic. We spent hours and hours building that world little by little, filling it with simple things, like a cabin in a tree, a beach covered with fabulous shells, a palm tree with sweet coconuts. But we also invented not-so-simple things, such as kisses that never lose their flavor, fantasies that are real, and love that survives the frosts of winter. In Calandria we chose what would exist. An illusion would never end unless one of us stopped believing in it. That was the rule. Another rule was that we had to laugh, or at least smile, to be able to live in Calandria. In case of sadness, one must depart to the other world and return free of sorrows.*

*He constantly talked to me about how beautiful Paris was, its cobbled streets, its glowing streetlights, the painters in the streets. One day I dared ask whether Paris could live inside Calandria. He answered yes. Afterward, I asked if Calandria could live inside Paris. He kept silent and then replied maybe. Finally, I dared to ask if one day we could continue dreaming of Calandria from Paris. He did not answer.*

*Wrapped in our fairy tale, we had managed to forget that the war was advancing toward the city. Absorbed in our love, enclosed behind walls, we almost forgot that another world exists out there. A world where there is often too much hate and too little love. But the sound of bullets made us wake up from our fantasy. The soldiers of the Khmer Rouge invaded Phnom Penh three days ago. Now, the war has finally broken into our lives. Everyone is afraid. They are emptying the city house by house. They say they are doing it for our own good, that the Americans intend to bomb Phnom Penh, just as they have been doing for years in Vietnam. But nobody knows the real intentions of these soldiers dressed in black. They smell like death to me.*

*Shots and explosions are heard in the street. At night the meow of cats is no longer heard in the background. Instead, an uncomfortable silence has spread everywhere. A silence only disturbed by a knock-knock on some door, followed by heartbreaking cries and bursts of machine gun fire. Then, silence again. The same story repeats, again and again, until dawn. I don't know where all the cats have gone. I don't know where I will end up myself. The French government is evacuating all French citizens. They are preparing a convoy that will allow them to leave in several helicopters and fly to Bangkok before flying to France. Some local refugees who jumped the fence are camping in the garden. They hope to be able to leave with the convoy. But the soldiers are only letting those who do not have Cambodian nationality out of the country. For now, they have stayed away from this house because it is considered French territory. I don't know how long they will respect the rules of war, for they don't respect the rules of life already. I'm scared. Not for my life, which I already consider as lost, but for his. What saddens me the most is that when the soldiers storm in, they will destroy our Calandria. There was still so much to build in that world.*

*His father has been talking on the phone for several days, in permanent contact with Paris, trying to organize the repatriation of the thousands of French people who still reside here. We breathe moments of anguish, and not even the aroma of lotus flowers can ease the anxiety of the uncertainty. He has promised me that he already talked to his father about everything. He has convinced him that our love is not something temporary, and that he needs me to leave the country with them. I believe him. He says they will hide me among their belongings in the trunk of their vehicle when they leave tomorrow for Pochentong Airport. They have diplomatic status, so they think the soldiers will not dare to search the vehicle to see if there are Cambodians inside, trying to flee. But I do not believe that these soldiers respect any rules now, and I fear that if they find me, they will harm them. If that happened, I would never forgive myself. He has a future ahead of him. I have never had one. I have managed to know happiness in these last three years, and I am grateful for it. I am ready for God to lead me back to the destiny He had already planned for me.*

*Just before writing these last lines, his mother entered my room and found me crying on my bed. In all these years we never talked much. She has always treated me with respect, but I felt that she considers me an inconvenient stone in her son's path. They never surprised us together, but I know they suspect what is between us. When she entered my room, I thought she was going to ask me to forget everything, that it had been a fantasy of young people, that I should follow my own path just as they should follow theirs. I thought she came to stop me from joining them in the vehicle. I thought she would tell me that I should put her son's happiness before my selfishness of being happy with him. And you know what? All those words would have made sense. It is what a mother who loves her son would have done to preserve her own happiness.*

*But today, she made a gesture I never expected. She sat next to me and, drying my tears, as if she were my own mother, she looked me in the eyes and asked me, "Do you really love my son?" I hesitated a few moments because I did not expect this. Finally, I answered yes. Then she hugged me and told me that now I was like a daughter to her and that I would leave for the airport the next morning hidden in the car. We embraced each other for a long time, and we cried together. I don't know if it was because of love, because of fear, or because of both. In those brief minutes, I felt closer to Paris than ever. I even naively believed that maybe I would escape my destiny and become a city girl, go to school, and even talk with a distinguished accent.*

*Then, when leaving my room, his mother crossed paths with him and they looked at each other in a strange manner that I was unable to interpret.*

*Afterward, he asked me why I was crying. He wanted to know what his mother and I had talked about. But I did not want to answer him. He stayed with me for a few minutes, hugging me, caressing me, telling me that everything will be fine, that we will soon be in Paris, that we will have a wonderful future surrounded by lotus flowers. The fantasy he described to me is a thousand times more beautiful than I could imagine while reading those stories to learn French. I made a decision. Tomorrow I will not cross that wall hidden in their car. If there is something I do not want to lose in this life, it is him. Tomorrow I will jump the wall by myself and return to my life pulled by oxen.*

*Goodbye, Mother. I just wanted you to know that I have discovered what love is, nothing more than that. If I survive what awaits me on the other side of the wall, I will continue to cultivate the lotus flower, month after month, year after year, until maybe one day he will sit at my table again.*

# CHAPTER NINE

## PHNOM PENH

Coming down to earth was inevitable. That first morning, in Phnom Penh, we held the second round of negotiations between the World Bank and the government. We had prepared several presentations suggesting reform packages for the consideration of each ministry. It was the turn of the health team to propose to the Ministry of Economy and Finance our ideas on what could be improved in the health sector. Bram, the director, had flown in from Bangkok for the meeting. He looked belligerent and ready for battle. I, on the other hand, felt ethereal and different. Bram always liked to have a pre-meeting to make sure we were all on the same page. He chose a breakfast meeting, something I hate because I am not caffeinated by then.

"I want uniformity of criteria," he said, looking at me.

By *uniformity*, Bram really meant that I was not to go off on a tangent and was to let him do the talking. I nodded, my lack of caffeine matching my level of conviction. Daniel, the chief economist, accepted Bram's plan — which wasn't really a plan, but an order— while his subconscious surely dictated that he would straighten things out later, when he left, in his own Latino way. Despite the transcendence of the memories, I couldn't stop thinking about Louis and all the magical moments we had lived aboard that dream-filled cruise. Once more, feeling you replaced in my thoughts by another man triggered an internal alarm, which, fortunately, was quickly silenced by Bram's rallying cry of, "Let's go!"

We arrived at the Ministry quickly. The streets had regained a certain sense of calm, although the rolls of barbed wire used by the riot police were visible on every corner, ready to be deployed, if necessary. We met in the same room. The projector was ready to show the government how to govern. The minister entered, together with his assistants, and with ceremonial courtesy he shook hands with each one. Without further delay, we proceeded with the meeting. The minister was anxious to know what our proposals for reform were, as if looking for a way to rescue himself out of the mud in which his party had become mired.

Bram began to describe our first proposal: expansion of the number of beneficiaries eligible to receive assistance to pay for health expenses. In Cambodia, health care was not free and, although the rates were not very high, for the poorest even a modest fee could lead to what it is known as "catastrophic payments" that might leave the family bankrupt. To prevent this, for some years, the government had adopted measures to protect the lower classes, granting exemption from payments to the poorest. These subsidies were, of course, largely financed by the development agencies. But only ten percent of the population received the exemption, and the World Bank argued that the quota should be extended to twenty percent to include a segment of the population that is almost equally poor and therefore deserves to receive such benefits. This was our first proposal, and it logically meant a greater government budgetary allocation for health care. Bram presented the reform, showing several slides with calculations we had made about the additional cost to the government, as well as the positive externalities that this measure would bring, such as greater domestic savings, which could in turn result in greater investment by families in education.

At the end of the presentation, the minister exchanged a few sentences in Khmer with his advisors and, without much enthusiasm, said, "We'll think about it."

We expected a more elaborate response from the government, or at least some hint of excitement. Bram, Austrian and methodical, went on to describe our second proposal: improvements in the quality of health services. Through our own studies, the Bank had managed to evaluate the ability of doctors and nurses who could make accurate diagnoses. The main conclusion of the report was that less than a third of the health staff could recognize basic diseases such as malaria or pneumonia. This result was alarming, as it meant that many lives were being lost due to misdiagnosis and incorrect treatment. Therefore, one of the measures proposed was a greater investment in the Faculty of Medicine. The minister, again showing little enthusiasm, objected with, "A too long-term measure. We will think about it."

Bram gave me a sidelong glance as if to say, "I warned you." I returned his look, replying, "If everything we did was short term, we would be at the same point in the long term."

Without further ado, Bram presented our third proposal, the most controversial of all: pharmaceuticals.

But as soon as the minister saw the word *pharmaceuticals* on the slide, he said, "We already made it clear that this issue was off the agenda."

That was the point where, forgetting more than twenty years of diplomatic experience, of saying things like, "That's an interesting point" while really meaning, "But what the fuck are you saying?", of agreeing instead of denying, of being someone else instead of me, I couldn't help it anymore. "With all due respect, your Excellency, what are you willing to talk about?" I asked.

Bram's eyes almost jumped out of their sockets. In an urgent effort to quell the rebellion on board his ship, he intervened. "Minister, I apologize on behalf of my colleague, who might be affected by jet lag."

I replied, "That is true. I apologize, I am experiencing some drowsiness, likely caused by the monotony of my colleague's voice."

Bram turned then from his usual pearly white color to the crustacean pink his compatriots adopt on the beaches of southern Europe. Even the minister himself could not help but disguise a childish smile when he noticed this transformation. To calm the situation, the minister suggested a break of a few minutes.

"Can we meet in my office, please?" the minister asked.

"Of course, your Excellency," Bram answered.

"Sorry. I would like to speak with the doctor alone, if you do not mind," the minister replied.

Bram's face then went from crab pink to the dark garnet of a barbecued lobster.

The minister's office was huge, with high ceilings, sober walls, and a cold feel that gave it the aura of the anteroom of death. Standing at the wide window overlooking the

Mekong River, the minister, with his back to me, was looking at Phnom Penh while I sat on the sofa and waited my turn.

"Do you smoke?" he asked me.

I said no, and he, lighting a cigarette, said, "Me neither."

He continued looking out the window, taking long puffs on his cigarette. He took off his suit jacket and loosened his tie. Without turning, he said, "Believe it or not, Dr. Gipani, there was a time when I bathed in those murky waters. The strange thing is that they did not seem so murky then. This city has changed so much... In our formidable swamp some enormously horrible buildings have grown, and the worst thing is that many of us have been trapped between them."

He continued looking out the window, as if time belonged to him, because it did belong to him. For some strange reason, the minister ceased to be a minister and became human, and I felt that this was his moment of truth.

"You know, doctor," he said, "horrible things have happened to this country, terrible things, and I do not speak only about the war. At least during the war we knew who our enemy was, but now... now we don't know... and we've all changed so much. But you... you remain the same, as much of an activist as the first time I saw you entering through that door. Your commitment to the cause is worthy of my admiration. Congratulations."

I didn't think I had ever been so flattered in my entire career.

"We are all prisoners inside our own walls. Me too," I answered.

"I know, I know... don't think I don't know," he said as he settled on the sofa. "But, doctor, I believe your walls are of another nature: not made of stone, but of a heart that has become stony."

I would never have expected such a personal response, one that referred to my love life. In another context, perhaps with another minister, I would have viewed that comment as inappropriate, but we had spent so many years engaged in that eternal game of chess that even the marble figurines had become of flesh and blood.

"With all my respect, Mr. Minister, I think this disease affects us both," I said.

The minister lowered his head, and I felt that I had put him in check. He remained silent, perhaps cradled by some ghost of the past and, then, looking me straight in the eyes, not with his deadly official look but with a new mortal human one, he said, "You may be right."

He served me a cup of tea in the ceremonious Asian manner and said, "You may believe that because of my position I have the power to change things at will, but believe me when I say that we are all bosses here with the permission of the big boss. And that one—" He interrupted himself just in time. "If I could, I would not hesitate for a moment to change this battlefield for another one, perhaps a greener one where I could breathe better. You just visited Angkor. Would you not say that the air is fresher there?"

His eyes drilled into mine, and I felt invaded. If I was reading correctly between the lines, his comment could mean that the state apparatus had spied on my movements in recent days, including the time I had spent with Louis in Angkor! If I was right, he was probably even aware of my meeting with the activist Boupha. How I should answer very much depended on whether my assumption was correct or not. But it was risky to assume that he was aware of my conversation with Boupha, and, even if he was, it was risky to venture that he knew that I knew about his past. It was an equation with several unknowns, which I decided to solve by maintaining the same degree of ambiguity.

"I imagine we all have a choice in life," I said.

Without delay, and with a now incisive look, he declared, "No, not once you pull the trigger!"

My heart froze. I felt that the equation now only had one unknown. Perhaps it was pure paranoia, but the truth is that I was disturbed to think that the minister could know that I had information about his past. I held the minister in high esteem, but Cambodia was always a country known to operate in a secretive manner, and only a few years before, political purges were the order of the day. Barely daring to look him in the eye, I got up and went to the window, where I looked at the Mekong. My knees were shaking, although I tried to disguise it as well as I could and tried to transmit some self-control. This ministry was not our building made of steel in Washington, where everything, starting with the temperature of the environment, was carefully controlled. This was a minefield, and I had walked into it.

Tentatively, I said, "If there is something over which we have no control, it's our past." And then I added, "But the future is today."

The minister got up from the sofa and advanced toward me. He also looked at Phnom Penh from the window. After an awkward silence, he said, "The future,

Dr. Gipani, is out there, in the streets; here only the mud remains ... mud, and a past made of mud."

"I think I should go back to my team," I said, as if asking for permission.

The minister nodded, and I walked to the door. Just before I opened it, he called me again. "Doctor. I want you to know that in the shadows I'm still working to make Cambodia a better place."

I hesitated for a moment, not daring to say what I really wanted to say. But finally, with the door already ajar, I turned around and revealed, "And she thanks you for that. With all her heart."

The minister nodded and uttered an almost imperceptible "thank you" that was a great relief to both of us.

I left him contemplating the world from the window, immersed in a stormy past that remained his tormented present.

When I returned to the meeting room, Bram was pretending to read some reports, but I knew he was only trying to hide his anger about not having been invited to the minister's office. That was an offense for which he would never forgive me. I returned to my position at the table and prayed that the minister would not be late. Ten minutes later, he reappeared and, with his team, sat down before announcing, "Good. Mr. Bram, please, let's continue with the presentation."

"Thank you, Excellency. Well," Bram cleared his throat, "let's move forward with the following reform proposals, and let's give the government time to elaborate a response to the previous ones."

Bram gave me a reproachful look as he made the last part of the statement, but the minister was quick to answer. "No. You will have my answer now."

Then, the minister, addressing me with a tender look, added, "You have my word that things will change."

The rest of the session evolved favorably, although naturally with its ups and downs. After all, it wasn't Christmas time either, when one could write a letter to Santa. But, in general, Bram understood that sometimes being genuine pays dividends. The minister felt like a human being again, and I had been reconciled with myself once more. A satisfactory result for everyone.

After two days of not seeing Louis, I had started to miss him. Worrying. It was easy, even comfortable, to have him around. We decided to meet at the FCC that night. But that place reminded me so much of you that it was like putting a stranger in our bed. The evening presented itself with gusting winds and a deceptive moon. He came still carrying the notes of the last interview of the day and a number of pencils without tips. Who the hell uses pencils these days? I asked myself. I suppose it was part of his retro appearance. He arrived disheveled, very French, and in a state of impeccable disorder. With his dashing air of furtive seducer, he filled my glass before sitting down, and made a toast, saying something esoteric that I didn't understand but that sounded more poetic than the rest of my working day.

To match his lyrical tone, I said, "I was thinking about your statement... I don't agree with you."

"Thanks." He smiled. "Which one?"

"With most of them," I answered, "but especially with your opinion that in love there is no future, but only the present."

"Look at us," he said, amused. "Are we not enough evidence of that?"

"I'm still in love," I answered, "and you?"

His eternal smile fell to the ground, breaking into a thousand pieces. He composed himself again quickly, though not fast enough to hide that behind that magic curtain something else was going on. But since I was never the kind of person who likes to read the last page of the story ahead of time, I decided to bring other lighter entrees to the table.

"What do you want to be when you grow up?" I asked.

"Younger," he replied.

"Me too," I said, "so that I can grow older again."

But just as I was about to plunge into a myriad of mystical phrases, I noticed, sitting at the bar, my friend with whom I enjoyed the most colorful night of fantasy at the funfair. She wore a dress looser than the last time, with less eye-catching heels, and without those hoop earrings that turned her ears into a circus trapeze. She was also missing her gaudy makeup and tigress talons. She was dressed less like a whore, in short. She was accompanied by a man in his sixties, who wore a floral print shirt half unbuttoned, exposing a thick gold chain and gray hairs on his macho chest. The minute she spotted me, she waved her hand, jumped off her stool, and started moving in my direction, screaming like a madwoman, "Friend!"

She hugged me tight, lifting my skirt in the process and scandalizing half the bar. She whispered loudly in my ear, "I'm getting married!" I assumed her decrepit companion was the beneficiary of this commitment, and my heart sank. As I turned to assess him once more, I saw that he was watching us with a creepy smile and teeth as yellow as cheese. When he also winked at me, my revulsion became irrepressible. She, looking at me with a big smile, said, "You see? I have also known love."

For some inexplicable reason, I felt like that helpless creature's guardian angel. I felt obliged to save her from emotional suicide. I was horrified to imagine her being seduced by that old pervert, her youth —or what was left of it— used to the last drop of sweat only for her to be abandoned one morning with a child in her womb. So, surprising myself, I did something very unusual for me, something that was quite worryingly becoming a habit in the last few weeks: I was spontaneous.

I stared into those alabaster eyes, reaching that place where the soul resides. I then walked my thumb and forefinger along the length of her young heron's neck, feeling her pulse accelerating at her throat. I placed my palm over her velvety nape and sensed her neck turning elastic. Gently, I pulled her toward me, making it clear that I would brook no arguments, until her glossy lips were so close to my mouth that her sweet wine breath invited me to drink from them. As my own life seemed to move farther and farther away from me, and it had been a long time since I too was gone from myself, I began to massage her lower lip first, as if this were a huge slice of orange and I a hungry pilgrim.

There I entertained myself, taking my time, recognizing the new textures, appreciating the nameless sensations, savoring the unprecedented flavors of her vanilla. Since I knew that a lesbian kiss was unlikely to occur twice in my life, I decided to rejoice in that lesson of unknown love. I ran my fingers along her jawline, committing her facial features to my mind, where she revealed herself as a beautiful nymph. An unexpected warm blizzard added a rebellious sensation amid that act of sedition. Fully immersed in the moment, I discovered myself licking her tender chin. After some more playful kisses, I drew back from her. I saw that her eyes were not closed with passion but wide opened, like those of an owl that just discovered affection.

"If he can kiss you like this, then marry him," I proclaimed.

Her frosty eyes became two gloomy lagoons, and all their warmth condensed in salty waters that overflowed those bottomless basins, down those mossy valleys, terminating at her chin. She took two short steps back and then escaped from there in a hurry, but not before saying a faint thank you. This would be the last time I saw her. Meantime, her companion, who had followed the whole production with great enthusiasm, dashed toward me in a threatening manner, as if demanding an explanation of why his fiancée had run away. Louis, acting as my shield, much less poetically than usual, said, "Get closer and I'll kick your ass."

Wrapped up in laughter, we walked along the riverside toward the restaurant where I had made the reservation. On one side, along the road, a tide of motorcycles flowed like a single body of red lights; on the other side, along the river, the fishermen's barges sailed in the dark, making themselves noticed only by the quiet sounds of their two-stroke engines. The night was marked by an indecipherable spell; the humidity of the environment wanted to speak, and the full moon, crowned with its halo, wanted to speak too. Even the muted shadows seemed to be willing to reveal something. When we arrived at the restaurant, Louis became silent.

"Have you been here before?" I asked. He shook his head.

It was a colonial house of solid walls and a sober façade, which with its lemon exterior and greenish wooden shutters reminded me of the Mediterranean. It was impossible not to unleash the imagination and travel back in time to the golden colonial times. We sat on the terrace, where the jasmine climbed uncontrollably up the mud-brick walls and an artificial fountain brought freshness with its sound of running water. There were six round white wrought-iron tables and, on each of them, a shallow glass vase in which a pink lotus flower floated. Louis ordered a double whiskey that he drank in one gulp and then ordered another one just before the waiter turned around.

"This whiskey has no future!" he protested.

The waiter smiled, thinking that maybe it was some Western joke and, recognizing that Asians are generally incapable of appreciating non-Asian humor, he proclaimed, "You are very funny, sir."

Louis thumped his glass on the table, causing a ringing metallic sound that drew the attention of the diners around us.

"I'm not funny, nor do I want to be. I repeat that this whiskey has no future!" he shouted. "I want to see the manager right away," he added with false calm.

The waiter, confused, hurried inside the restaurant, and a few seconds later the manager came out at a brisk pace, looking horrified, with the bottle of whiskey in his hands and with the waiter following him closely, chasing his shadow. It looked like a scene from a cartoon. The misfortune made the manager stumble over a tile, and the bottle was thrown into the air before it shattered on the floor with a disruptive clangor. Everyone was appalled by the massacre of that old whiskey, which both the manager and the waiter mourned dramatically.

"Just what I said: that whiskey had no future." Louis said, impassive, taking another long drink.

After that surreal incident, the scene gradually regained some sanity, and Louis, after proving to himself that he was right, and with two double whiskeys already in, looked more at peace.

We ordered a bottle of wine and I proposed a toast: "To the success of your future novel."

"Thank you," he answered with his glass high. "Although... surely nobody will read it."

"Why do you write about love then?" I asked.

Louis took his time to answer, and, meditatively, he inhaled the vapors of the wine, as if trying to distil its soul too. He replied, "Because it brings me closer to it."

In my life, I had met very few men willing to talk about love; not about their feelings, but about love as a theme per se. Yet for Louis it was a fascinating obsession. I could feel by the tone of his voice how he considered that venture a path toward the discovery of some superior truth, perhaps to the ultimate solution of most afflictions. I found that aspect of Louis intriguing, even inexplicably erotic. I had no doubt that almost any woman would feel that way too.

"What I don't understand though is—"

"Why am I alone?" Louis finished my sentence.

The waiter returned with excellent timing and, in addition to bringing the first course, proved once more that the Asian sense of humor could never marry the Western. He said smiling, "Sir, the fish *amok* has no future because it's already dead."

Louis, completely ignoring the Cambodian bad joke, replied to me, "Actually, I'm not alone, nor do I feel alone. I just think that not everyone is made to live as a couple."

"But you believe in love..." I ventured.

"A lot. And surely I think more of it than most of those who go on throughout life thinking they are in love. Simply, I believe that there are many dimensions of love, and I have chosen to live in one of them."

"The one of sleeping with a different woman every month?" Hastily I added, "I'm sorry. I shouldn't have said that."

Louis took refuge again in his glass before getting lost in a point in the infinite, while I cursed myself for having started the conversation with such a blunder. Then he continued: "The conquest of your body has been pleasant, but the exploration of your mind has been the true delight of this trip."

Coming from almost any other man, I would have judged his words as the tools of an experienced womanizer. Yet I believed him.

"But... you would choose not to live with me for life," I answered.

"To avoid losing you forever," he swiftly answered.

"Because life as a couple is a loss, according to you."

Louis seemed to have reflected long and hard on the subject and had all the answers at hand. "I don't need to be loved," he answered, "I want to feel in love."

I couldn't deny that, for the kind of love Louis was referring to, time is what saltpeter is to metals: a potent corrosive. But it was difficult for me to accept that someone refused to surrender to the natural evolution of love, accepting and even embracing each and every phase as a distinctive season of the year, without missing the heat in winter, nor the cold in summer. In other words, without being human.

I replied, "I recently read a novel. It was about two good friends who take a trip a tiny island in the north of Mozambique that resembles a medieval fortress. Suddenly, both find themselves trapped in a fantastic past in which they are taken prisoner in some parallel reality. The sole condition to regain their freedom from their medieval guards is that they must write the most wonderful love story ever told; otherwise, they will remain on the island forever. The story they must invent must also be autobiographical, so they themselves must live their own love history right there.

"They try to fall in love with each other by all means. They stroll along the white sandy beaches, holding hands, arms around the waist, stroking each other's hair, collecting mysterious shells with fabulous shapes and telling each other that a whisper of love lives hidden inside each of these shells. They admire each sunset tinted with magnificent reds as if it were the last. They gaze fanatically into each other's eyes as if it were the first time and, while they observe each other, they make confessions that they rehearsed with no conviction, but which were so poisoned with love that they took them as a sign of such. They drink sparkling rosés and sugary cocktails to sweeten every moment of their present, when in reality a simple glass of water would have refreshed them more. They strive every moment to immerse themselves in deep conversations, when often a shallow silence was what they most desired. They made love with bravery, defying the rules of physics, loud like ferocious wolves, as if encouraging each other, when a simple tender kiss and a modest 'I love you' would have given them more pleasure.

"The years went by and, finally, they managed to write, or rather to pretend to write, a novel that resembled a passionate romance. And, just before handing it over to their guards to recover their freedom, they look into each other's eyes and discover that a long, a very long, time has passed, and that out of their daily friction some sort of affection has been born: an affection that, although they are unsure whether to call it love, they are now not prepared to let go. They feel indivisible. And do you know what they do then? By mutual agreement, they throw the novel into the sea and decide to stay there forever, imprisoned in their new source of freedom."

Louis floated in my story for a while, perhaps imagining himself imprisoned, maybe released, on that very same island. Then, more on principle than by conviction, he said, "I guess love evolves just like seasons do. One has to accept each season for what it is and enjoy winter for its cold, summer for its warmth, spring for its flowers, and autumn for its leafless sunsets. But as much as we would like to stop time and eternally admire those flowers in full bloom, the reality is that its beauty is ephemeral, and in its ephemeral nature resides its beauty, just like love. I'm not blind, I know the wisest course would be to accept the annual calendar just as it is. But... what can I do if I was born in the month of May?"

I couldn't deny the fact that the first poems are the most dazzling of all. But love is more than just those few first verses.

"Trust me," I said, "I myself lived the most charming and magical love story that two lovebirds can possibly experience. We spent not weeks or months but years intoxicated, levitating in that ephemeral love that you so fear to lose, and yet I wouldn't change a single one of those first floating days for the sensation of feeling him as one more part of my body: irreplaceable."

Louis meditated again, and, without much inspiration, he said, "Maybe not all of us are built for that kind of love."

"You're wrong, I said, looking him straight in the eyes. "You're very wrong. And I am about to prove it to you. But before I do... excuse me. I need to go to the restroom. Do you know where it is, by the way?" I asked.

"Yes, at the entry way, climb the stairs to the first floor. It is the second door at the end of the hall," he answered without even looking at me, focusing instead on reading the back label of the wine bottle.

I remained seated, watching him, until Louis realized that I was still there, unmoving.

"I thought you were going to the bathroom," he said.

"And I thought you've never been here before," I replied. "How do you know where the restroom is?"

That was the precise moment in which his gaze transformed into a lagoon of dark waters, and from them, past ghosts that had never entirely drowned suddenly emerged. Louis's façade of alabaster turned into adobe, which dissolved in a rain of tears. Louis was finally revealed as made of flesh and bone, fallible and sincere: a child.

I gave him a few minutes, and then I asked, "You know this house well, do you not? It is the former residence of the French consul. And you are..."

"His son," he finally confessed.

"And she was..." I continued.

Louis kept a bitter silence before finally revealing, "She... she was Thida. The only love of my life."

Louis, who had sat with his back to the restaurant, turned then to contemplate —now as if feeling liberated— his old home. He lost himself there for several minutes, hearing, I imagine the echoing voices, watching the unchained ghosts, contemplating the ruins of his history, smelling the fragrances of the past, and, above all, trying to decipher that last conversation behind the door, Thida and his own mother's, the day before fleeing Cambodia.

"Nothing looks as clear as life seen from outside," he said.

Then he plunged back into his memories, seeing himself defoliating daisies in some corner of the patio. He pointed to the window and said, "That was her room. And here is where I would sit to take my accordion class, an instrument I always hated until I noticed that she used to spy on me during my class; then I started to find pleasure in playing for her. I made a promise that I would teach her to play the accordion when we lived in Paris. In Paris! Imagine... From Paris to a common grave under who knows what rice field..." He sobbed out his words before succumbing to deep and bitter tears, not caring that others saw him while he fell apart.

When he finally regained some of his composure, he opened his heart fully. "The worst thing is that my mother died without me believing her. She spent half her life insisting that, that morning, Thida jumped the wall because she decided so herself and not because she incited her to run away from me. But I always suspected that my mother, wanting to break up a relationship that should be considered impossible and harmful, convinced her to run away during that conversation they had in Thida's room just before I entered. I spent the rest of her life blaming her for Thida's death... and, in a way, of my own too.

The morning we fled Cambodia, they had to force me into the car to go to the airport for our evacuation. If they had not, I would have stayed here, like her, ready to accept the same fate: death. There wasn't much difference between dying of a bullet to the chest or having my heart torn apart —a spiritual death from which I was never resurrected. I spent all my youth looking for her. In college, while my classmates would spend their time making love in the park, I spent all my free time locked up in the library, documenting, writing useless letters to all organizations that supported the exodus of genocide, corresponding with embassies, following clues that always turned out to be mere mirages. Before the appearance of new technologies, this type of search was like trying to find a needle in a haystack, and by the time the Internet was a reality, the needle was lost forever among a thousand haystacks. I have searched through all the files that exist on the genocide, I have traveled to all the refugee camps in the region and outside of it, I have even sent messages in bottles, released messenger pigeons, and left appeals in each pagoda of each village of this damned country. I have never stopped looking for her, because although I have long assumed that Thida was lost in time, if I interrupt my search, I would become lost myself too.

He stopped looking at that point in infinity where his eyes had been stuck and said, "Do you understand it now? I don't need to love another woman, because I'm still in love with her."

Surprising myself, and expecting a no for an answer, I asked, "Do you want to show me your house?"

He hesitated a moment and said, "I swore I would never set foot here again, but I also swore to find her, and I didn't."

Against all odds, Louis got up, and, with authority, he took me gently by the arm to escort me through the gates of his sadness. We climbed a spiral staircase that connected the second floor with the attic, and there the door to his mysterious past opened wide. Everything was in place as if time hadn't passed: the white lacquered desk with its hinged wooden lid; the Montblanc pen with its silver nib and the sharp-tipped Faber pencils; the walls papered in pastel cyan, with thick frames displaying photographs of the past; the bedside table also lacquered in white, holding a clock with stilled hands and a copy of *Madame Bovary* by Flaubert; his single bed, with its goose-down duvet and the pillow filled with impossible dreams. Everything was still there, intact. Even the spirits.

Sitting on the bed, not like the adults that we were but like the teenagers we were not, Louis grabbed my hand, which no longer felt like the sturdy one of experienced captain but rather like that of a cabin boy. He looked at me with sheepish eyes instead of his usual wolfish look. I noticed how his pulse accelerated, inexperience and a cold, almost glacial sweat reduced his infallible instincts of a successful hunter. Trembling and doubtful, he approached my lips, which received him asleep, and moving hastily, he awkwardly placed both hands over my breasts. He then laid me on his bed, impregnated with ancient memories, and began to kiss me along my neck, frenzied and without rhythm. I doubted whether this was really Louis, or a juvenile version of him.

He fumbled with the buttons of my blouse, and when at last he gave up his one-handed attempt to undo them, he ventured unsteadily under my blouse to fail twice to undo my bra. When he finally did, he didn't know what to do with so much unbound flesh. As a raw recruit in the battle for love, he rested on me, crawled through the deep trenches, and, hardly knocking on the door first, he slipped inside me, rough and lumpy. He groped between the soft areas, but he was unable to touch a single one of the magic keys that he had pressed before when composing the most furtive and harmonic melodies. Finally, his passion culminated in a stony moaning that too closely resembled puberty. I didn't even get close to any ecstasy.

# CHAPTER TEN

## PART SIX: PHNOM PENH

Now I knew that Louis and I had something in common: an unattainable love, a ghost. Until last night, my vision of love lived in the antipodes of his. However, with that last revelation everything changed. Louis and I were —for different reasons— two poor souls afflicted with a coronary syndrome. In some way we denied ourselves the opportunity to love again. Maybe due to some false conception of disloyalty, or perhaps to continue feeling attached to something, to someone, who existed as a concept rather than in flesh, but certainly safe from the daily erosions that destroy love itself. We both embraced that ethereal matter for a common reason: to dodge solitude.

Unconsciously, I took myself to Louis' old house, now converted into a restaurant of shadows and whiskeys without a future. "He is inconvenient," I kept telling myself along the way. Louis was inconvenient, and my growing attraction to him was not only weakening every day the umbilical cord that joined me with you but a new one was also emerging between him and me, and that is something that terrified me greatly because I was accustomed only to belonging to myself. But the last days had been so intense, so lyrical, so magic and intoxicating too, that now it was difficult to cleanse his scent from my own skin. Maybe, as he himself admitted, Louis was not marriage material, but ... wasn't that precisely what I needed at that moment in life? The love Louis could offer was probably nothing more than a marvelous cotton cloud, a hot air balloon, a fabulous sunset —an ephemeral feeling, in short. But if love had any advantage at our age, it is that by the time the afternoon was ready to project its last sunbeams, our own heartbeats would also be reaching the sunset. In other words, there was no time to mess it all up.

Once at the restaurant, I sat at the same table where we had dined the night before. A strange timeless sensation suddenly overcame me. I discovered a huge magnolia bearing magnificent flowers that had gone unnoticed during the previous evening. I thought of Louis as a young man, under that euphoric tree, devouring hardback books, writing poems of soft verses, looking sideways at the window above with the hope that she was watching him, as she watched him from that same window, wishing he had noticed her from below. "Being noticed by someone..." The beginning of the end of loneliness... Each table was still adorned with freshly cut lotus flowers, which still brought with them the dew imported from the pond. I wondered if this scene, so carefully decorated and so early in the morning, was the work of the woman sitting under the stairwell, which seemed to serve as an improvised office space.

After a few minutes spent enjoying that garden and my circular thoughts, as no waiter came to take my order, I decided to go up to her to order a cappuccino without sugar, without cream, without chocolate powder —a mirage of a cappuccino. The woman, a Cambodian with warm hands but frosty eyes, was battling against hundreds of ungovernable bills while listening to one of those radio stations that broadcast music from the good old times. She looked at me over her glasses and said, with an unexpectedly American accent, that they were not really open yet, but that she hadn't wanted to disturb my moment of glory and that's why she had let me enjoy the garden. She offered to prepare something for me herself. Grateful for the kind gesture, I politely ordered my coffee and waited in front of her office, because it felt inappropriate to make her bring it to me all the way to the garden.

While she was preparing the coffee, I entertained myself looking at the many small old photographs that were stuck against the wall beside many tiny watercolors of lotus flowers. They were photographs of other times, happy photographs, all of them naturally sepia-tinted and from French postcolonial Cambodia. One photograph in particular suddenly attracted my attention. It was one of a young boy playing the accordion while seated next to a young woman. Something in his face sparked my curiosity. I stretched my neck to see it better, and my heart sank when I recognized Louis' eyes. At that precise moment, the woman came back with the clink of a coffee cup. I apologized for the intrusion. "Old photographs have always fascinated me," I excused myself.

She smiled. "May I tell you a secret? These photographs have not really faded because of time, but because of the abuse of looking at them constantly."

I faked a smile. But in my mind there was only one thought: was that really Louis? My heart and breath turned stony. I had the overwhelming premonition that that could indeed be him, and, that the woman seated next to him, who was in front of me at that moment, was the love of his life.

"Excuse me," I said, "I know what I'm about to ask you won't make any sense but... by any chance... are you named Thida?"

Her smile turned bitter, and she replied, "No."

I felt an inexplicable and profound relief, and I turned in the direction of the garden, trailing the nervous tinkle of my coffee cup.

Before I reached my table, I heard her voice again. "Although there was a time when I was..."

I could not breathe, and, instead of pausing, I accelerated my pace toward the garden, the chiming of my soul adding its voice to the tinkle of the coffee cup. I took refuge at my table, sitting with my back to the house, and let my eyes fill with tears as salty as the Dead Sea. As if trying to justify my own crying, I tried to convince myself how wonderful it was to have found the missing link in that chain the Khmer Rouge once broke. Before I could come to terms with the discovery, I noticed the slow footsteps of the woman behind me, crunching the gravel in her wake. She settled down beside me, and also with a bell ringing inside her heart, she asked me in an almost imperceptible whisper, "Do you know him?"

I hesitated for a moment, torn between repairing that broken chain or joining my own link to it. Finally, my more human side made me nod. It was then that her eyes became two lagoons so opaque that they seemed crystalline, on which a rising sun flashed the glimpse of a lost future. We avoided looking into each other's eyes, perhaps to delay until the inevitable the question that we were both concerned with. But, finally, I narrated how Louis and I had met on that cruise, just two weeks before, omitting how we had talked to each other, how we had walked holding hands, how we had kissed, how we had made love; omitting everything. At the end of my story, a sincere comment escaped directly from her heart: "On a cruise... who can survive that..."

With considerable effort on my part, I hastened to clarify that we were not together. But then, she looked at me with a half-moon smile, and said, "Don't be offended, dear, but, if he's still half the magic man I once met, right now you're probably there, dying of fear, hesitating between staying with him or running far, far away, because anyway, whatever you do, you will regret it for your whole life."

She had hit the nail on the head: it was just the way I felt.

Then, Thida, the woman resurrected from the past, told me how her story went on from the chapter that was closed when she jumped the wall.

She had nowhere to go. Her biological family no longer existed in her heart; her adoptive family would soon be on a flight back to Paris; and her native Cambodia had also disappeared at the hands of horror. She wandered the streets, literally bending around each corner in search of her new destiny. That was while the soldiers kept emptying the city. She begged on the roads in the direction of Kampot province, where she had heard that the Khmer Rouge were more benign and didn't kill without question.

In her narrative, she limited herself to saying that horrible things happened to her, without specifying. "Horrible," she said over and over again. Fortunately, for the Khmer Rouge soldiers, there was little doubt that she belonged to what the Angkar called *old people,* the real rural Cambodia, without links to modernity: the Cambodia the new regime intended to restore. That kept her alive. But she spent several years digging irrigation channels, in swamps where malaria and typhus threatened to take her with the black crows.

Finally, after the liberation of Cambodia at the hands of the Vietnamese army, the nightmare ended —although others would continue forever. Later, with the arrival of the United Nations mission, as she had an adequate command of French, she secured a position as interpreter with the peace mission. And, later, in gratitude for the services rendered to the UN mission, she managed to enter the special visa granting plan for those who had lost everything during the war. Thida changed her name and claimed to have lost her entire family to the genocide. She justified her actions by telling me, "That was the death and rebirth of the country. Mine as well." For that reason, Louis lost all trace of her in his desperate search. The residence visa she obtained would send her to the remote state of Wisconsin, in the middle of the United States, where she was under the tutelage of a couple without children, both academics at the University of Madison, who paid for her education. Finally, she came to study translation and interpretation.

For the next two decades of her life she worked as an interpreter for various international organizations, including the United Nations, in New York, where she met many sensational men, skilled in languages, and in the use of romantic words, but all with an insurmountable and common defect: they were not Louis. Eventually, the International Tribunal for the crimes of the Cambodian genocide was established to do justice to the victims of the Khmer Rouge. She did not hesitate for a moment to join as an interpreter.

When I asked her if she ever tried to find Louis, she replied, "I did. My way. I bought this house, and, as promised, I continued cultivating the lotus flower, wishing that one day he would return to sit at my table." I looked around and saw that the entire house was sown with that fabulous flower.

Thida explained how her life was always marked by those initial years in this dollhouse. She also confessed how, mysteriously, she never found herself alone later in life because his everlasting memory became a blanket that provided warmth and calm in the cold nights. Thida added that, in the eternal waltz that life is, she never felt as though she was without a dancing partner, and the world —her inner world— just kept spinning and spinning, whirling golden memories all over, just like shooting stars. Thunderstorms would always remind her of Louis and how they used to make love outside in the garden while getting soaked by the love that fell from the clouds in the form of rain. Later, during her days in Wisconsin, the summer storms did nothing but bring those memories alive with every clap of thunder, with every lightning bolt, with every flurry.

But perhaps what I most sympathized with was her description of the characteristic scent of prophetic man, which used to impregnate her skin for days after each encounter. The day before she jumped the wall, she asked him, chimerically, to spray one of his borrowed clothes with his own aroma, which she treasured for life under her pillow, allowing his scent to seep into her dreams. "I looked for this unique scent on the chests of various men. Always unsuccessfully," she confessed.

And I blushed when she looked me in the eye and admitted that she could barely concentrate on her bills when she sensed Louis' scent infused in my own skin. I felt sorrow for her. There is nothing worse than a whip of jealousy. When she eventually finished with her narrative of her life after jumping the wall, she revealed to me, "I still don't know if I did it out of love, or fear."

Surprised that she hadn't questioned me about what he and his life were like, I asked her if she was not curious to know more about Louis. She then asked, "Does he still have the ability to caress a woman throughout the entire night?"

My uncontainable blushing gave me away. She displayed a smile tinged with bitterness, which she swiftly tried to disguise by saying, "I never expected him to become a monk."

After a prolonged awkward silence, each one trying to avoid the central question as much as we could, I ended up taking the risk by asking, "And what do we do now with this mine that we just have stepped on?"

Then, Thida replied, adding some humor to detract from the drama, "Let's do what women have traditionally always done: let him decide."

I said goodbye to Thida and, with my mind still floating in unsettled emotions, jumped on the first *tuk-tuk* that passed by. I went searching for Louis where he mentioned he would spend the morning interviewing another survivor of the genocide. I felt most divided. On the one hand, I felt the moral obligation to tell Louis about the tremendous discovery I just made. I was thrilled with the idea of being able to stick together two pieces of film that life and tragedy had cut in two. Perhaps the romance of their lives could go on in the most unexpected cinematic way. The very idea of seeing happiness in Louis' face when I announced the existence of Thida filled me with excitement. Yet that would surely also mean the end of our short film; a brief episode that, despite its uncertain end, I must admit I had begun to consider as the first chapter of a story to which more pages could be added. Another crossroads, another bittersweet irony of life that, once again, proved that everything related to the game of love is a gamble. The *tuk-tuk was* not moving fast enough in the midst of the internal acceleration I felt. But finally, we left the city behind and arrived at that sinister place on the margin of humanity: the killing fields.

The extermination camp is a place of conflicting feelings, where the relief and calm brought by death contrasted with the intense suffering that we know preceded it. It looked like any other random field on the outskirts of town. It would actually have gone unnoticed had it not been for the explicatory placards, the mass graves, and the small pieces of bones still scattered and semi-buried. It was impossible to ignore that just three decades before, on that random plot of land, the systematized extermination of more than a million Cambodians had taken place. They were brought in trucks, in the middle of the night, to find death —also peace— at dawn. You could still hear their quiet prayers while they waited to be executed by clubbing, to be beheaded with palm leaves, or, if fortunate, killed by a bullet to the head. Each massacre, a ritual, that often took place while loudspeakers played loud music so that the screams of agony would not alert the inhabitants of the surrounding villages, who surely sensed that those meows didn't come from the cats but from the children who returned to the other world in the company of their families. Had it not been for the little signs the government had placed there to describe the different phases of the terror, or for the monument in its center, where thousands of skulls were piled up in huge towers, no one would have ever presumed that the small pieces of cloth and bones that surfaced when the earth was removed were not the leftovers of a Sunday barbecue but the memory of dehumanized humanity.

I spent some time walking among the tourists, who wandered downhearted and head-down, as if feeling ashamed of their own human condition. The crying of the youngest Westerners could also be heard upon their realization that their rosy lives on the other side of the ocean scarcely resembled the hardship of the real world. Finally, I found Louis. He was sitting under the shade of an acacia, interviewing a local man of advanced age, who kept gesticulating in a flamboyant way. Louis noticed me in the distance and made a discreet gesture. I waited for him to finish with his interview. I enjoyed contemplating him in his role of journalist and writer. He looked enigmatic and sublime, enveloped in an aura very much his own that portraying him as what he was: an allegory. And then I asked myself: what if…?

Fortunately, I didn't have enough time for that internal pendulum that fluctuated between my heart and reason to begin swinging again. Louis said goodbye to his interviewee and greeted me with a warm hug. But a moment later, the Cambodian returned in his quest to deliver a document he had forgotten, and Louis reacted with a gesture of disapproval that seemed strange to me. After a brief exchange of cryptic phrases, Louis dismissed him courteously but with haste. Before leaving, the old man said goodbye to me with an unexpected comment: "With your hands, miss, you could well be an *Apsara* dancer."

Louis began to speak with a strange voice. Somehow nervous. Out of nowhere he confessed to me how therapeutic the night before at his old house had been. He said that he felt connected and at peace with his own past. Something sounded unconvincing. He said he felt reconciled, serene, and even released from the love cage that had held him captive for too long. He said he felt like a new man. "I think I can even love again," he said, looking at me with all-powerful eyes that triggered my defenses. The suggestion would have made my knees shake had I not felt a terrifying hunch.

Perhaps led by the surrealistic feeling of being wrapped up in a fantastic story where the dead resurfaced from the past, one after the other, I asked, "Who was the interviewee?"

Louis was upset by my question. After the eloquent speech about his resurgence from the ashes, and his new capacity to love beyond dawn, I imagine he expected the reciprocal release of my own feelings, or some revelation that made him anticipate what I felt for him. But he quickly realized that I wasn't ready to let him go off topic. He bowed and, embarrassed, confessed, "That man is Saroun."

"Saroun! Saroun the love of Sopheara, the dancer you interviewed in the floating village!?" I exclaimed.

Louis nodded, but the way he did so, without any joy, warned me that he was hiding something. Inquisitive, I asked again, "You already knew he was alive, right?"

Louis explained that he had some evidence that that could be the case, although no real proof. The story we heard from the chief, Sopheara's current husband, was therefore indeed true. He helped Saroun escape the camp instead of executing him as he was ordered. Sopheara's husband had freed Saroun, risking his own life. An extraordinary act of bravery!

I cheerfully exclaimed, "It's wonderful! I can already imagine Sopheara's joy when she finds out that the love of her youth is still alive!"

But while I was floating in my own happiness, Louis remained impassive. "I'm glad as well," he replied, "but it isn't my mission here to unite what the Khmer Rouge separated."

"What!?" I shouted. "What are you talking about!? You have the obligation to let them know!"

"As a matter of fact... No, I don't. My job is to document stories, not to change the world. I am not the World Bank, Gipani," he answered firmly.

I was stunned. I couldn't believe that Louis didn't feel morally obliged to share this information with Sopheara, a woman trapped in a life, and even in a marriage, in which she didn't belong.

"But just imagine—" I started to say. "Imagine you were Sopheara, wouldn't you like to know about the existence of the love of your life?"

The irony was that there was indeed nothing to imagine. The love of his life, Thida, had also survived the genocide! And I was the only one who knew about it. It burned me to know. I had rushed up there to reveal to Louis the fact that Thida was alive, but now he himself was denying that very same information to others. It would have been too easy, perhaps too unfair as well, to pose the simple question at that precise moment — "Wouldn't you like to know?"— and let his stubbornness resolve the problem of my life. Afterward, all I would have to do is just let things follow their natural course, which, by the look of it, surely would guide him toward me. Yet if I was to win him, I wanted to do so competitively, thus, I took a different approach.

"You must tell him. It's just a matter of symmetry. Now, that man, Saroun, knows about her life, but she doesn't know about his," I argued.

Louis looked away but remained silent. I scrutinized him, and then asked, "Because... you've told Saroun about her, have you not?"

Louis gave me a look that clearly indicated that he had omitted that essential information from his conversation with Saroun. And that's when I lost it. I fiercely reproached him, telling him that there was something deeply twisted and even sick in his way of doing things; that he was trying to prove his own love theories at the expense of people's lives, those whose happiness had been lost by a cruel past.

"Gipani," Louis calmly said, "think carefully about the implications of what you propose. Would it be fair that the chief, who risked his own life to save Saroun, would now see his marriage ruined by our meddling? Would it be fair to awaken in Sopheara's mind the false dream of recovering Saroun so late in her life? That glorious past is a fougasse that no longer exists, other than in their hearts, and, it is there, and only there, where it should go on."

"That's a lot of bullshit!" I shouted "I can't believe you just let that poor man walk away, depriving him of an opportunity to love again!"

I went on, railing against him. I told him that not wanting to play God was also playing God. I told him that I didn't understand his distorted vision of love and all that discourse in which he wanted to live in a permanent state of falling in love. I even suggested that there was something sadistic in his attitude of not wanting to reveal what he knew, and that it seemed like some kind of rejoicing or revenge because he himself did not find his Thida.

Louis cut me off. "Saroun did not even ask about her!"

That revelation certainly surprised me.

"Why? What do you mean?" I said.

Louis explained: "Saroun told me about how much he loved her and about the fairy tale in which they lived immersed. But, even though I explained that I was investigating a number of genocide survivors and that I was interviewing others, at no time did he ask me if I had information about whether she was alive, about her whereabouts, or about what her life currently was like. And that's where you can read between the lines that Saroun also prefers to keep her in his memory and not in his reality."

"That's your own interpretation. I would definitely want to know. And if I could reconnect with the person I loved all my life, and whom I still love intensely today, I wouldn't hesitate for a moment to do so," I recriminated.

Then it was Louis who said something that took me completely off guard. "Do it then. If you really still love him, as you say you do, why don't you just talk to him? Or... are you not being completely sincere with yourself?"

My inner castle suddenly collapsed. Touched, and with not much conviction, I said, "It's not the same."

"It is; it is the same," he replied. "Gipani, we both regard the ephemeral side of love with horror; we both fear time and the implacable erosion that time has on love. And for the same reason we both stopped looking for love within our reality, because, unconsciously, we feel the only way to preserve its beauty is by keeping it in our imagination."

Louis was probably right. But I refused to admit it. Instead, I walked away and jumped on a *tuk-tuk* towards the city, frightened. I wandered the streets of Phnom Penh, chasing your spirit in every alleyway, on every balcony, in every corner; telling myself, "Look, this is where he told me that fantasies are only such when one of the two stops believing, and that they become a reality when the two desire them with equal intensity. And, look, that same boat, *The Kanika*, is where we dined, alone, and he said to me, 'How strange that there are no more tourists on board, don't you think?' when he had secretly booked the entire boat for us so that nobody would disturb our magical moment. And look, that's the purple color of that shirt of his that made him so irresistible." Everything reminded me of you. All. But, in the end, I had no choice but to face an incontestable truth: that you were the past.

That truth —a leaden and insurmountable reality, an unpalatable bitterness— had also become a heavy burden for me, which I kept dragging through life like an impossible jumble, like the relic of the past that we were, like the trophy of our extinct glory. We were a winter that would never be a spring again. Sad as it was, that's how it was. On the other side of the Mekong, however, there was Louis: a new lighthouse, a new spring. But, as one more proof of the cruelty of life, just when I had almost resolved to cross the river of my inner fears, an untimely ghost had emerged from the murky waters: Thida. And then I said to myself, "It's her happiness or yours."

Later in the day, I called Louis and asked him to come to the restaurant where we had supper the night before. He was initially surprised by my sudden change of mood, and also by my insistence to meet in what once was his own home. He accepted the proposal. He arrived resplendent with a white linen shirt, navy blue pants, and tidily disheveled hair —the perfect Mediterranean writer. He brought with him a copy of the book *Letters to a Young Poet* by Rainer Maria Rilke, and a masterly opening sentence on his lips: "I'm only interested in the invisible."

After an ephemeral kiss that I dodged by presenting the corner of my lips and that he interpreted as a false truce, he sat with his back to the restaurant and ordered a bottle of Viogner, to which the waiter answered, this time with the right humor, whether he wanted it with a future or without it.

"With a lot of life this time," he answered.

The patio was illuminated by numerous tiny candles, adventurous fireflies, and large glowing glass spheres hanging from the almighty magnolia, all of which created an enchanting atmosphere. The lotus flowers continued to adorn each of the six little tables, but this time the flowers were an unusual green: the color of hope. With the first glass of wine, Louis proposed an enigmatic toast: "To our tour around the world. From where do we begin the conquest?"

Surprising myself, I answered that I wished to begin the journey from Cherwell Boathouse, the legendary pub on the river in Oxford, where you and I used to drink endless glasses of Pimm's on summer afternoons. At that precise moment, I realized that you had become a wonderful but also hefty anchor, which I was getting ready to release to the bottom of our ocean. Louis took the initiative, and grabbing the pole of our punt, he began to paddle safely while lyrically describing how the ocher leaves fell along our serene navigation over the waters; how words were barely needed for us to communicate because our glances revealed everything; how the swans with their cotton feathers escorted us, feeling envious of us for being the newcomer river princesses. By the time that dreamy boat reached the shores of England, enveloped in sublime verses and subtle strokes, the first bottle of wine was already a memory, as were my feline defenses.

"And now?" he asked.

I was then the one who, assuming control of the rudder, sailed at cruising speed until we reached Île de Gorée off the coast of Dakar, where we arrived at midnight on board an ancient merchant ship, wrapped in one of those enchanted and fluorescent indigo-color mists the Sahara likes to drag along with its moist breath. Louis watched me, enraptured, listening to my story with more poetic than common sense, presumably feeling fortunate to have found a lover who was willing to put one more step on that lunatic ladder to the moon. And when I finished telling him of our wandering among the multicolored houses of that island under the starlight, he asked, with that look so characteristic of him, "Where have you been all this time, Gipani?"

With excellent timing, the waiter returned, asking, "Is everything all right?" I answered his question silently: "I wish it would be." He uncorked a second bottle of wine, this time red, and I knew that in it we would end up drowning the two of us.

Music that resembled that of an old jukebox played in the background, bringing us Frenchified melodies from the colonial days. I thought that, for some reason, the past sounded better than the present: more romantic, more exotic, even more erotic. I think the symphony had the same effect on Louis, who lost himself in an intimate trance while stirring the wine in his glass, before saying in a low voice, "There is a place called Ilha, a place that lives in my imagination, and my imagination lives in it. It's a fantastic place created to invent fantasy, in a world where an excess of realism often stifles magic. In Ilha, you grow and grow, until one day you're ready to conquer the (other) world. Then, the whole world becomes Ilha."

I stared at him, mesmerized, and thought that one day I also treasured a similar world, but later modernity gradually took me away from it. And, even more tragically, I moved away from myself as well to become a tool in the service of that same damn modernity, devoid of all sensation, of all magic, of all. I think that was one important reason you and I perished as "us." It wasn't so much the succumbing of the couple but the capitalization as each of us as individuals.

At high risk of being swallowed in the well of nostalgia, I hastened to go on with Louis on our fantastic journey around the world. I suggested we travel to a place on the Cambodian coast: Kep. We arrived in the middle of the night, in the middle of a tropical storm that made the coconut trees tremble, with lightning intermittently illuminating the ocean. We arrived after several hours of driving, in which the deepest conversations had been mixed with the most trivial laughs, in a cocktail of fruity feelings in which the sugar meets the pepper, awakening contradictory and novel sensations. Floating in that intoxicating sensation, we didn't wait to dive into the sea. The waters were warm, and the thunder was retreating, although the nearest islets continued being illuminating occasionally among the mercury waters as if they were ships adrift. In that enchanted atmosphere, we embraced each other in the sea, making sincere and slow love under a dreamlike sky.

"There must be a pier in the story!" Louis interrupted. "There must be one of those long and discolored gray wooden piers that go deep into that sea of mirrors. Because that way, upon awakening from that fabulous night, I would discover you seated at the other end, with your gaze fixed in the infinity, no longer you but the one you really want to be. And you would discover that I'm not myself either, but the one I once was. We would walk along that long walkway to the unknown with only one hope: to find ourselves together at its end. And we would walk while remembering the moment we met, shyly. A shyness that condensed into timid words; words that made us sigh among the candles; sighs due to how magical it so early on felt that cruising together to the abyss would be; a cruise that we couldn't make in that initial moment, because we were anchored to other realities but which we wished time would grant us. As it did.

"And in that walk along the pier, we would thank life for it, and ourselves too, for having believed in such a dream, for having trusted ourselves. And in that slow but inexorable walk to the other end of the dock, I would remember one by one every phrase we confessed, every lingering glance, every sigh of hope and hopelessness at the same time. Already at the other end, the mist would become thinner and scattered, and from it a *dhow* would arise, one of those Arabian sailboats, this one painted in pink: the color of fantasy. And, then, the boatman would say, 'If you're ready, come on board. Life is yours from here on.'"

Never had a declaration of love had the shape of a boat. For the first time, I seriously considered walking that last stretch of my real life together with Louis. But choosing him was also choosing to live with the ghost of his memories. To deny Thida the opportunity to be reunited with her usurped happiness would also haunt me for life. I feared that our life together might become a house full of ghosts, which only the specter of love would eventually inhabit.

During the whole soiree, I had been observing Thida, hosted in the shadows, who I presume was barely breathing while waiting to find out about her own future. I looked at Thida once more. Her destiny was in my hands.

In the distance I noticed how the frosts on her eyelashes had begun to melt with the possibility of a new spring. I understood then that love is like magic: invisible, unpredictable, charming. I realized as well that in love —as in magic— you have to believe; believe, and, above all, let yourself be a little deceived. I looked at Louis, dazzled by the flame of the candles, and it all became clear.

I calmly got up and stood in front of him. He placed his head against my belly while I stroked his curly hair, massaging his neck and allowing myself to feel the drumming of his temples in my being. Thida, meanwhile, observed us, waiting helplessly for the resolution of her own destiny. She stared at us passively in the gloom while her gaze alternated between darkness and the sparkling of hope. I would venture to say that even in the days of the Khmer Rouge camps, she didn't fear as much the fate of her own soul. With Louis's head still wrapped in my hands, pressing it against myself, I asked him what we would do if past ghosts returned from love. He muttered, lethargic, confused, "Ghosts don't love; that's for the living only."

"That's right," I told myself, "only for the living..." For the living like him and me, but also for the living who managed to survive death thanks to love: to the living like Thida.

I continued caressing his wheaten hair, although this time my strokes had the touch of a farewell. And then I said, "Since I met you, magical realism finally makes sense. But now you must remain magical, and I must return to reality."

There was no doubt: he was a wonderful lucky idiot. After his spring of one thousand flowers, he was about to embrace the warmest autumn. I then stared at Thida, who correctly interpreted my signal as the thaw of her infernal winter. The ice in her eyes melted, pouring down her chin to the ground, giving birth to a carpet of fresh moss leading all the way up to him, the love of her life. It had taken thirty-eight years, thousands of nights, and only God know how many sighs to reach that moment. And, then, I thought that it is magic, and not reality, that should be seen as valid in the affairs of life. Before I finally detached myself from Louis, he looked up and sensed it all. He knew instantly that at the end of that dreamy pier there wasn't me. With the acrimonious smile of one who reticently accepts that the journey has come to an end, he muttered something unintelligible that I interpreted as a tacit goodbye. With short steps, I withdrew from him, exiting his life forever.

I didn't turn around to see what happened next. Nor have I ever had any contact with Louis again, or with his magical world. I don't know how his story ended, although, in my mind, I have imagined as many endings as life permits: all. In one of them, she approached him, calm, placed her hands on the back of his neck, and time rewound as if it had never run. In another ending, after an epic reunion, time eventually alerted them to the fatality of time itself. But out of all my many conjectures, I choose to believe that their love remained preserved as what it was: a beautiful state of mind. Thus, Louis, after a few minutes, paid his bill and left there never to return, while Thida dismissed him in silence, terrified to sully in the present what she so candidly lived in her heart. This is love: a gamble with one single beginning but infinite possible endings.

Sometime later, I found Louis' novel in a small bookstore in Washington, D.C. I confess that I studied that book line by line, always trying to find, in every word of every sentence, some indication of our wonderful days together in Cambodia. It makes me happy to believe myself described behind those turquoise nails, at the end of that pier in Kep, or in his last sentence, as simple as it is certain: "Love is easy in difficult times and difficult in easy times."

Printed in Great Britain
by Amazon